The Queen of Clocks
and Other Steampunk Tales

edited by Crysta K. Coburn

Cover art and design by Bess Raechel Goden.

ISBN: 978-0-692-12533-5

Contents

Introduction

I have always loved tales of the fantastic, and I think it's safe to say that appreciation is shared by many in the steampunk community. Among other things, steampunk is an imagining of worlds that could have been and might one day be.

The same can be said for fairytales. While they have never been unpopular, fairytale retellings, whether fantastical, modernized, or turned into science fiction, are currently enjoying a particular popularity. So, I thought, why not combine these two vibrant and creative worlds into one? Enough fellow authors were equally delighted by the idea, that you now see this book before you.

Like the tales upon which they are based, the stories here run the gamut of light to dark, short and long. Bess Raechel Goden's *The Clockwork Nightingale* and K. Gray's *The Little Wind-up Mermaid* are very different takes on stories by Hans Christian Andersen. *Oddysey?* by Aaron Isett (an updated version of Homer's *Odyssey*) and *The Marionette* by Phoebe Darqueling (inspired by Carlo Collodi's children's novel *Pinocchio*) look at what haunts our darker sides. *Sleeping Steaming Beauty* by Victoria L. Szulc, a re-imagining of a classic tale covered by both Charles Perrault and the Brothers Grimm, draws parallels to our own time and locale. *Treasure* by myself and the title story *The Queen of Clocks* by Thomas Gregory are both based on tales recorded by Brothers Grimm (*Snow White* and *The Poor Miller's Boy and the Cat,* respectively) and maintain a traditional fairytale flavor.

I hope these tales entertain you, dear reader, as much as they have me. It was a joy to work on this project with everyone, and every contributor has my deep and abiding thanks for going on this journey with me.

Crysta K. Coburn
May 2018

The Queen of Clocks
and Other Steampunk Tales

The Clockwork Nightingale

by Bess Raechel Goden

A long time ago, when magic was just beginning to give way to reason and machines were still called "inventions," there was an emperor who ruled over China. This emperor had a great love of beauty. He sought long and far for the best fruits, the most intricate golden trinkets, and the softest velvets. After a time he built himself quite a collection of fineries. It became large enough that when he was presented with new delights offered by exotic merchants, he offered to show them two or three better items from his store in return. This became his passion, and he was eventually known to his people as the Emperor Who Had Everything.

One day, he ventured down to the vaults to recount his most prized rarities and passed two of his serving girls along the way.

"She sings so beautifully, it's not like anything I've ever heard before," said one girl to the other.

"That is a big compliment coming from the girl who sneaks into every concert held for His Majesty," replied the other, who giggled. Upon noticing the Emperor eavesdropping, however, she stopped abruptly and gasped. They bowed low,

1

afraid he might punish them for idleness.

"Arise girl, I am not angry. Indeed, I am glad you enjoy my splendid concerts, for they are certainly the best in the country. But tell me, who sings even more beautifully than my performers, I wonder? I should like to meet her," said the Emperor to the shaken servant.

"Your Majesty, I would be happy to take you to the meadow where she makes her home. If it pleases Your Majesty to follow me, I will take you now. It is not far beyond the walls of the palace." And with that, the girl meekly led him outside.

It was not long until they turned onto a dirt path off the main road (which was, of course, the finest road in the land, made from steel and built to last by the Emperor's best blacksmiths). The Emperor's step faltered at first, as his soft and slippered feet were unused to anything but polished hardwood and metal. But eventually his legs remembered what to do on the honest earth as they wound their way through the tall, sun-dappled trees. The forest was so quiet that he could hear his silk slippered steps padding softly on fallen leaves.

Straining his ears as they advanced, he could just make out a few golden notes floating on the distant breeze. The sound grew louder as they approached, and now the Emperor could see why the forest was so quiet. Perched on a low hanging branch was a small and rather plain-looking nightingale, but what she lacked in visual beauty she certainly made up for in song.

Gathered around her, all of the forest creatures sat and listened to the beautiful tune. The notes took shape and intertwined, surrounding the Emperor in a softness more supple than any of his velvets. Each one seemed to glisten in the setting sun, ten times brighter than any of his golden trinkets. The honeyed melody made the Emperor feel a sweetness he had not tasted in any of his finest fruits. The song ended and the listeners lingered, hoping for more, until the continued silence reminded them of their mundane duties, and one by one they made their way toward home.

All except the Emperor. He stayed until the audience had dissipated and then approached the nightingale with tears in his eyes.

"You moved me, little bird. Something that all my gadgets and fineries have never done! I should like to take you to my palace. I will build you a golden cage, feed you the best seed from a jeweled bowl, and let you sleep on silken pillows, if you will sing for me."

The nightingale regarded him for a moment. Then she hopped cautiously onto his shoulder and rubbed her soft head against his cheek, drying the tears that had collected there. He smiled, but was not surprised. His royal nature was as unused to disappointment as his royal feet were to walking the dirt path which they followed back to the palace.

And so the Emperor thought his collection was finally complete. He kept his newest prize in a golden cage and let her out to fly as she wished, though he always kept her bound to the cage with a fine silver chain, lest she fly off to another man's collection.

While the Emperor seemed happy, so did the little bird. She glowed with love when her throat filled with song, and the whole palace rejoiced in her beauty. The Emperor made her sing almost every night, inviting guests of all sorts to envy his catch. She became the talk of the capital. Some even came from neighboring kingdoms to listen to her captivating song.

In fact, the little bird grew so famous that a renowned tinker decided to make an homage as a gift to his majesty. He worked night and day with the finest silver wire and rarest gemstones to finish it, what many would call the masterpiece of his career. It was a little clockwork nightingale, beautifully crafted, with swirling silver patterns on a background of gold plates delicately hinged together and lined with the smallest diamonds, sapphires, and rubies even the Emperor had never seen. It sang, too. When you wound up the small golden key underneath its right wing, it sang the loveliest tune. Some said it was just as lovely as the real thing. It could only sing one song, but the Emperor never seemed to grow tired of it. He was so pleased with the little toy that he played its tune over and over, until the whole palace was singing it.

He played it so much that after a time, he forgot to ask the real nightingale to sing. She became sad and restless at his neglect. She would watch the sun rise and set behind the shimmering bars of her gilded cage. Perching her soft head on the hard bars to try and catch some of the rays on her beak, she would think longingly of the sweet breezes and her favorite perch that she had once called home. Eventually, she could stand it no longer. She snipped the silver chain with her beak (it was really her love of the Emperor that had kept her there), and she rode the sunset back to her beloved meadow.

It took the Emperor some time to realize that the nightingale had left him, but when he did, he did not mind. His toy sang for him whenever he felt like playing it. And it was so beautiful to look at. He believed himself content.

Though, as the years went by, he made the toy sing so often that its song began to beat unpleasantly against his brain. Everywhere he went, he seemed to hear the song echoing behind him. One day, the toy's gears wore down and cracked with overuse. The tinker came to repair his creation and made it sing once again. Yet now when it sang, the tune sounded tinny and hollow. No trills, no variations, no differences, no joy. He soon grew disgusted with it and wished that he hadn't neglected his little bird so much. How he wished to feel her sweet notes dance in his ears once again.

His heart saddened, and eventually the Emperor became ill with regret. He began to miss her so much that he gripped the clockwork nightingale day and night, but never again wound the key. The Emperor finally took to his bed, still gripping the toy imitation of his little friend. Sometimes he squeezed it so hard that the ornate filigree left bloody impressions in his palm, as if he could lend some of his life to this metal mockery of what he had lost. The best doctors attended him, but no remedy could be found. He was very old by now, and his councilors decided that it might be best to start looking for his successor. Visitors stopped coming by to see him, as his court became more concerned with impressing the next emperor. He grew sadder and lonelier.

Then, one night he received a visitor he hadn't wished to

see, the one visitor no one wishes to see. When he came, the Emperor sighed and said, "Perhaps it is time. Perhaps there is nothing, no one left for me here."

Death bent low, a small patch of moonlight illuminating his bony smile. But just before his last breath was whisked away from him, the Emperor glanced at his windowsill. He saw the little nightingale perched there, watching him with sympathy.

"Oh, my little bird," he said, his voice cracking with joy, "please sing me a song before I die. I have longed to hear your sweet voice ever since you left me."

The nightingale smiled, and love seemed to pour from her throat as she sang such a beautiful tune that even Death stood up to take notice. She sang to the Emperor of her meadow; of the sunset glowing through the trees; of the breezes that stroked her feathers when she flew; of the twinkling starlight that pointed her way back to her soft nest. And then, suddenly, the Emperor knew that no matter how long he searched, he could never possess everything of beauty in his collection of fineries.

And as Death listened, he felt something, too. It was a longing that grew from deep within his bones, something he'd never felt before: a longing for the touch of sweet breezes and sights of starlit branches. Enchanted, he stood and listened until the bird ended her song. The longing had grown so insistent within his bones that Death felt that he must see such beauty for himself. He forgot all about the Emperor and wrapped his dark cloak around himself, then melted into the shadows and was gone.

"Oh, my little bird, you saved me! I know now why you left. It was your love of the meadow that filled your heart with song," said the Emperor, tears glistening on his cheeks.

The real nightingale, the only nightingale, fluttered over to the Emperor and perched on the now tarnished and warped golden toy in his chapped palm. She lent her soft head to his cheek and wiped his tears away, just as she did when they first met. He smiled. She sang with joy. The Emperor closed his eyes and listened. He wondered how he could have ever valued a lifeless gadget over such a sweet reality. And as he was serenaded to sleep, he let the mangled clockwork nightingale slip from his fingers and shatter on the floor.

After a time, he grew stronger – strong enough to return to his throne. He never again asked the nightingale to stay, but she would come to see him anyway from time to time. And when she did, he made sure to relish the beauty in every note, since he now knew that the most important things in life were never meant to be possessed.

Sleeping Steaming Beauty

by Victoria L. Szulc

For many years all had been well in the United Kingdom. Queen Victoria and Prince Albert ruled a world where the sun never set on the British Empire. But after Prince Albert died unexpectedly, the Queen suffered a demoralizing depression, yet hid it from her subjects.

She acquired the best of every segment of society from scientists and sorcerers to mathematicians and magicians. The combined strength of the scientific and mystical brought an extraordinary advancement and prosperity. Some members of the court developed incredible weaponry, machines, and technology. Others excelled at higher learning and spiritual gifts. With these powers behind her, the Queen continued to conquer the whole world and managed her territories by offering parcels to certain good subjects.

King Stephen and Queen Layla of New London, distant cousins of the Queen, were awarded a large portion of the former France. Per the orders of her majesty, they were to procreate as quickly as possible to help keep the Queen in power over all. Queen Layla was soon with child and word spread throughout their land that loyalists would be invited to the christening.

However, not all were pleased with the Queen Victoria's ruling of the planet. Many had not been invited to join the Queen's consultations. Some outright refused. Still others became unwilling victims of progress and were forced into industrial slavery or servitude.

One such person, a sorceress named Malena, had been pushed aside when control of her forested land was awarded to the rulers of New London. She was forced into work at a brutal industrial factory where they fused her torso with equipment in order to make her work faster. They clipped her wings and replaced her horns with metallic replicas. When separated from nature, her abilities were diluted and Malena couldn't cast spells and escape.

For two months, Malena endured torture and was nearly worked to death. But one evening, the factory overheated. The boilers heaved and threatened to burst. The cooling system failed and left the building to fill with smoke. As humans around her began to choke, Malena tried to breathe only through her horns.

The foreman finally caved to opening the windows at the top of the factory walls. They were easily thirty feet high and figured no one would be able to escape. But when the toxins billowed out and fresh air was drawn in, Malena felt stronger than she had in weeks. Smoke sputtered from her horns as she climbed up maintenance ladders far from the wretched service floor. Yet when she reached the top of the roaring machines, Malena was still too far from the windows to get out.

With a brilliant stroke of genius, and the last bit of her strength, she ripped one of the failed ceiling fans from its mount, bent the blades, and fitted them to her wing nubs that poked just above her corset. She winced as the metal cut into her tender skin and then used the lacing to suture the fan pieces to her body. With a sigh of relief she wiggled the nubs and the blades beat wildly in response.

The bleating tones of the danger signals suddenly stopped. Foreman scrambled to get the slaves back to work as the building cooled. When her captor looked up, Malena glared at him.

8

"Close the windows! Now!" he hollered. As some of the workers ran to crank them shut, Malena beat her new wings as fiercely as she could and was soon flying. And just before the openings closed completely, she shot through the panes with her new metal appendages breaking the glass as she burst forth.

Shards fell around the disgusted foreman as the shadow of the sorceress passed the setting sun. The Queen would not be amused at Malena's escape.

—

Queen Layla rustled through her bedchamber. "Surely this was a mistake?" She hadn't been this nervous since she gave birth a week prior.

"No, Your Majesty, Malena escaped." The Queen's attendant shivered.

"And the King knows?" Queen Layla clasped her hands around a lace handkerchief and prepared to wipe desperate tears.

"Yes. He asked I tell you."

"Hmm, very well then. Tell him that no crier, no staff be allowed anywhere near her former property. Do it immediately. I am certain that she's returned there to regain her powers. I do not want Malena to hear of the birth of our daughter."

"Yes, Your Majesty."

As her attendant left, Queen Layla cringed. Her husband had been far too soft to rule over their small kingdom. Now their daughter's life was at stake. She prayed that the King would grow a spine for God's sake.

As she sat down to pat her eyes, the Queen thought she heard a flap of wings outside her window, but by the time she looked up, the large raven that had witnessed her conversation was already enroute to his mistress, Malena.

—

King Stephen addressed the court with a smile. The christening of Princess Aurore had gone splendidly, with each

9

honored guest bestowing gifts and well wishes. "And with the last of the gifts, I am pleased to announce our honored Fae: Velo, Verity, and Constance!"

Three tiny orbs twittered around the gilded bassinet of Princess Aurore. The chirp of Velo could barely be heard and the courtiers leaned in to listen. "I bestow on thee, Princess Aurore, the gift of beauty, not just of the skin, but of the heart, as well." Satisfied, Velo moved aside as Verity flew to the royal child.

"I bestow on thee, Princess Aurore, the gift of song, so that your lyrical words will inspire peace and happiness to all." Verity floated away to make room for Constance, but gasps filled the hall. The three gifted Fae hid under the child's blanket.

A tall shadow filled the doorway. "Oh, what a lovely party," Malena hissed. The guests parted in fear, leaving a clear path to the rotunda. Her mechanical wings clattered as she flew over to the Princess. "And a beautiful girl. Aurore, the name of the dawn. How fitting."

"Don't touch her," the King warned as he tried to hold Queen Layla back.

"Touch? Oh, my dear King, I'm here to give a gift."

"A gift is not necessary, Mal." The King attempted to soothe the sorceress.

"You call me Mal? As if you really know me? Well then, perhaps a curse?" Malena chortled, her mad laughter echoed throughout the room.

Queen Layla could not hold her tongue, and a barrage of haughtiness sprung from her lips. "So Mal, as in malnourished, malcontent? Are you offended then? That you, of all people, should be invited to where you obviously don't belong?"

"How dare you! I did belong. You took what belonged to me. Thus, I will take something that belongs to you." Malena leaned in towards the newborn princess. She was so furious that steam shot through her brass horns and startled the child. "Before the sun sets on the New London Empire on Aurore's sixteenth birthday, the Princess will prick her finger on a spinning wheel and die." The sorceress glared at the royals before the squeal of her mechanical wings pierced the halls of the castle. Malena shot through the doorway as the subjects of the court ran and took cover.

"Do something!" Queen Layla screamed at the King.

The Fae floated from under the newborn's cover. "Wait, wait. Constance still has to give her gift," Velo squealed.

"Yes, yes!" Verity cheered on.

"I can't take the curse away, but I can alter it." Constance soothed the child. "I bestow the gift of a good sleep at the approach of death. A sleep from which you can awaken, with a kiss from the truest of loves."

King Stephen held the Queen as she sobbed. "I want all the spindles in the kingdom burned immediately. All manufacturing of garments will be done by machinery from this day forward," he ordered. Soldiers and guards rushed from the palace and went to every home and business in the kingdom. By nightfall the glow from the fire of burning spindles could be seen for miles.

—

Over Fifteen Years Later...

"Papa, I'm going out to pick berries," Brass Rose called to her father.

"Be careful in the wood. I'm off to work, but be back before dark." Rose's papa hollered back as the young woman scurried out. He worried about the adolescent who truly wasn't his, but had raised as his own child since infancy. He gathered his tools and headed for the small saw mill. It was just a field away on his quiet property on the outskirts of New London.

Meanwhile, Brass Rose began to sing as she picked berries along a thick line of bushes not far from their cottage. She'd lived a very simple life with a good and pure heart. Her father had taught her most of what she needed to know. And what he couldn't teach her, three lovely Fae aunties did. Brass Rose didn't know that she came from royalty, or that she'd been betrothed the instant she was born. Yet she was happy and often

11

sang to the small animals in the forest.

On this day, one before her sixteenth birthday, Rose plucked plump berries for her cake that the Fae would bake later that day. As she pulled at the luscious blue bulbs, her sweet voice echoed around their property.

Normally, her songs only entertained the woodland animals, but a dashing prince, Phillip of New Paris, had decided to take a ride outside his usual territories. He wore a long riding coat and his top hat sat jauntily atop his head. He rode a mechanical steed, Maverick, that leapt over the earth with ease.

He paused and debated whether he would hunt, when he heard the most lovely song. He pulled on the steed's forward lever and headed towards the sound. As he approached the wood miller's cottage, Prince Phillip gazed upon a young woman he'd never seen before.

She wore a stunning blue velvet gown that enhanced the pale beauty of her skin. A brown corset beheld her womanly frame. Her curled locks were held up with ornate rose and brass combs. A few loose strands fell into her face as she leaned into the shrubbery.

The Prince was enchanted by this woman and wondered why he hadn't seen her before. So enticed was he, that his hand slipped the gear and Maverick lurched forward and steam belched from his nostrils.

Rose was startled at the noise and almost fell backward.

"Oh my lady, pardon my rudeness." Phillip dismounted in a hurry and rushed to Rose's side.

Rose had never seen a younger man before. The vision in front of her warmed her heart. "Oh, I—I, who are you?"

But her father had trained her to be cautious as she'd never know who might come to their property. She gripped the handle of her basket to be ready to pummel this intruder.

"I am Prince Phillip of New Paris." The young man had a swath of dark curly hair that sprung forth as he tipped his hat to her. "And you are?"

"Rose, Brass Rose of, well, um, here." She stuttered, surprised that she had earned the attention of a royal.

"And here is?"

"The sawmill property. My father owns the sawmill." Rose paused as perhaps she'd said too much. The Fae had always warned of divulging details. She'd only met a handful of the sawmill workers and a few families of the nearby village.

"I see. It's a beautiful place."

"So what brings you to this neck of the woods?" she tried to pry.

"I was going a bit beyond my boundaries I suppose. And I heard an incredible voice. Was that you?"

"Yes." Rose blushed. For the first time she felt different. Her feelings leapt around her chest like a box of frogs.

"Would you sing again?" Prince Phillip was enraptured. He'd quickly forgotten about his betrothed who he was to meet in two days.

"Yes." Rose began to sing a sweet tune and before she could resist, Prince Phillip had gathered her in his arms. They waltzed amongst the greenery without a care. Just before the Prince leaned in to kiss Rose, the familiar buzz of the Fae's wings tickled Rose's ears.

"Oh, I must go. Ever so sorry. I'll be late," she gushed.

"For what?"

"I—I can't say. I mean, not just yet. I have to make a proper introduction." Rose was suddenly aware that she hadn't acted like a lady and didn't want the Fae to know. "I will be here. Tomorrow perhaps?" She hurried off before the Prince could follow.

As Rose left, Prince Phillip was suddenly embarrassingly aware that he was engaged to someone else. "Let's go, Maverick." He jumped on his robotic horse, pulled several levers, and charged for home.

—

"But, I say, she must have a bigger bustle," Velo argued.

"Alright, I'll concede to the size, but not the color. She is Rose. The gown should remain pink," Verity rallied back at her sister.

"Ugh, you two! Do not spoil it for Rose," Constance chided them both. "Besides we need to get the cake in the oven."

"You talk as if I cannot hear," Rose complained as the three Fae alighted around her dress. "I do not understand all of this fuss for my birthday."

The Fae exchanged anxious glances.

"I know you're trying to make me happy. Well, today I found someone that made me feel exuberant," Rose gushed and twirled in her new gown as her father came in.

"Oh dear." Velo felt sick.

"What is this? You've met someone?" her father bellowed.

"Yes, Papa. A prince."

"Are you certain?" A look of horror crossed his face.

"A prince?" Verity and her sisters hovered in a panic.

"Are you sure?" Constance tightened her grip on her wand.

"Yes, oh my, he—he was lovely!" Rose plopped down on one of the simple wooden chairs.

"Fae, calm down. Everyone sit. We knew this day would come, only one day sooner than expected. Now is the time." The saw mill owner took Rose's hand. "Dearest Rose, I must tell you how much I love you. And how much your auntie Fae love you. But you are not born from my flesh. You were given to me to protect and hold dear with the Fae. You, my darling, are a princess in your own right, Princess Aurore of New London, and are betrothed to a prince already chosen by King Stephen and Queen Layla. On the day of your christening, your life was threatened, so your real parents entrusted your care to me and the Fae. I know that this must be a terrible shock for you."

"This can't possibly be true." Rose was devastated. She ran her hands feverishly across her silken gown as her chest heaved with sobs.

"It is true, Rose, and I am ever so sorry. This dress is to be your wedding gown, and not just a dress for your birthday. I was to deliver you to the palace tomorrow, but I am gravely concerned that with a stranger on our property, your life is at a greater risk. So tonight we will have a brief celebration here. Once nightfall arrives, we will head for the palace." He bowed before his charge.

The Fae twittered in positive response.

"Yes, tonight." Verity wrung her hands.

"It must be." Velo sighed.

"Yes, we should hurry," Constance chimed in.

"And what if I refuse?" Rose lifted her chin in a small show of defiance.

"You have no choice, Rose. You are known as Aurore. The kingdom is waiting for you. You have been its best held secret. I won't allow you to be taken or have the monarchy destroyed. I made a solemn vow that I must keep. Without our protection you will most certainly die." The owner of the saw mill stood. "My princess, let us prepare for your journey."

The cake was soon eaten, the gown finished, and all of Rose's possessions packed. Within an hour of nightfall, Rose and the Fae were hidden in a large steamer trunk underneath a blanket covered in straw in the back of a small carriage.

Unfortunately, more than Prince Phillip overhead Rose's singing. As black as the night that grazed its wings, Malena's raven had eavesdropped on the few hours of conversation. He hurried home to his mistress as moonlight shimmered on his silken dark feathers.

———

"You don't understand. I love this woman. She had the voice of an angel. It was mystical," Prince Phillip argued with his father King Hubert.

"My son, you are promised to one of the most important ladies in the world. And she is the destiny of New London. Your marriage will unite our territories. It was ordered by Queen Victoria herself. Tomorrow you will be present for her return to public life and servitude. Within a few days you will be her husband." King Hubert twirled the end of his handlebar mustache in anticipation.

"Not until I find out what happened to Rose." Prince Phillip rushed out of the extraordinary Hubert Manor with his father completely aghast at his bewildering behavior.

He rode off into the night with Maverick set at full throttle. The metallic beast thundered through the countryside until they reached the cottage. But the little homestead was dark. With a flick of Maverick's glowing eyes, two beams lit the cottage from the outside. The Prince stumbled in to find it completely deserted. "Blasted!" he cried and strode out to Maverick. Within moments he was off to New London. Maybe he could argue with King Stephen over his engagement.

—

Rose was stunned as she popped out of the steamer trunk and was then helped by soldiers in crisp red uniforms. She blinked at the glare of the bright lights of the castle. The Fae swirled around her in a dizzy fashion. The man she'd known as her father was given a proper military coat and stood at attention while servants whirled around them.

A crier entered with a crisp parchment in hand. "Your Majesties, King Stephen and Queen Layla."

"My child!" Queen Layla sobbed and embraced an entirely confused Rose.

"Welcome home, my darling." King Stephen hugged them both. "Come, let us get you settled in."

Rose's stepfather bowed as she passed him and followed her true parents. Her heart ached as the man she'd known as her Papa had curtailed to her. "I love you," Rose whispered as she was guided away. They passed several Victorian gilded halls and rooms before Rose was led into a spacious bedroom.

"My dearest Aurore, sleep well tonight. We have much to catch up on. There are guards outside to protect you and servants to cater to your every need. Good night, my darling." Queen Layla kissed the cheeks of her only child.

"We will see you in the morning." King Stephen gently

grazed her face.

Suddenly, the two monarchs were gone and Rose was alone in the room. She gazed out the window to New London. Thick clouds of industrial smoke billowed out of massive factories. Their hefty plumes blocked the moon and stars. No birds chirped. No trees swayed in the gently winds of the eve. She felt sickeningly overwhelmed.

A brief knock startled her and a servant entered. "Is there anything I can get for you, Your Majesty?"

Rose took a brief look around the room. The bed was immense, with fine tapestry curtains, and a fresh nightdress awaited. A small table, made of ornate carved wood, held snacks, a pitcher of water, and a pot of tea. There was even a private toilet. "No. I think I have everything," Rose stammered.

"Just ring the bell should you change your mind,Princess. Rest well." The lady's maid left with barely a sound.

Rose collapsed on the bed and cried. The dress she wore was the only familiar thing she had. She traced her fingers along the seams and smelled the magic of the Fae. She barely rested that night. Little did she know, there would be plenty of opportunity to sleep later.

—

King Stephen and Queen Layla consulted with the Fae. "No one else will be allowed in the palace tomorrow. We will have an intimate celebration for Aurore's birthday. Once the sun sets, we will send for King Hubert and Prince Phillip and commence plans for the wedding." King Stephen ran his fingers through his beard. "We will protect her at all costs."

"Of course." Velo smiled.

"Never let anyone in." Verity nodded.

"She's safe here," Constance chimed in.

"Very well then. We will see you in the morning." The King and Queen exited for their bedchamber as the Fae sat in the library. With a subtle nod, their help closed the door and left.

"Protected? Humph, I think not." Velo grimaced.

17

"Someone could get in." Verity shook her head.

"She's not safe here." Constance groused. "And I don't know if there's much we can do about it."

—

Prince Phillip galloped on through the darkness, his heart on fire for the young lady he knew as Rose. As he closed in on the palace, Maverick halted and reared as his sensors beeped.

Malena's raven swooped in and clawed at the young Prince's face causing him to fall off his steed and lose his blaster.

"Bastard!" He pulled for his sword and shield as the raven repeatedly dived in and around him. The bird's claws clattered against his metal defense while the Prince dodged and parried. Finally with a swift turn, he waved his saber high and spliced off the head of the wicked raven.

As the Prince remounted Maverick, a thunderous roar came from the grounds outside the palace. Immense vines thickened into brown weeds with gold tipped thorns that slashed his shirt and scraped his skin. They entrapped his body and pulled him high and away from his steed. Maverick galloped away into the darkness. As the thicket around him grew ever more dense, a voice echoed through the night: "You cannot save her. No one can." The cackle that followed chilled his blood.

Prince Phillip peered through his horrifying captivity to see a black figure fly to the top of the castle. As he slipped into unconsciousness, Malena was prepared to take over the kingdom.

—

The Fae fluttered towards Rose's room after the palace was plunged into darkness. The screams of servants and royalty alike echoed through the parlors and rooms.

"Not good," Velo groaned.

"Not good at all," Verity agreed.

"Terrible." Constance moaned with disgust. "We must hurry!"

—

As the thorns and brambles squeezed the palace walls, Rose sat upright in bed. The grandfather clock struck midnight and the chimes seemed to haunt her. With glazed over eyes, she looked about the room, then stumbled into the halls. Her pink gown dragged the floor as she strode with faint purpose to a particular space. The sewing room of the royal seamstresses was filled with lush velvets and intricate laces. Several machines were ready for production.

But Rose slipped past these pieces of equipment to a sizeable closet door. In her dreamlike state, she turned the knob to find the last old fashioned spinning wheel left in the land. She felt compelled to reach out to touch the spindle. It punctured her forefinger, and she collapsed into a heap upon the parquet floors.

—

Time seemed to freeze in the palace. All humans fought off an impending slumber much like one that had befallen Rose.

"We must find her, the spell has started. Damn her!" Velo cursed.

"Yes, Malena is here," Verity cried.

"That bitch!" Constance hollered as they flew through the halls. "The sewing room. She has to be there."

The Fae buzzed into the servants' quarters and hurried to their Princess.

"We need to get her to a bed," Velo urged.

"Yes, to rest proper," Verity agreed.

"And find the true love. Did she say his name was Phillip? Did she fall for the betrothed?" Constance questioned.

"Yes!" Velo chirped.

"Indeed," Verity enthused.

"Well then, let's lift her and find him." Constance started a spell. "With the power of wands of three, the Princess to bed, will find her be."

The three Fae tipped their wands at Rose, and with a bright yellow poof, Rose was sent magically back to her bed. The Fae arrived with her and laid her out as if she were peacefully sleeping.

"Outside, now!" Constance commanded and the three mystical beings flew out the window amongst the thicket.

"There he is!" Velo shouted.

"Yes! Over there." Verity pointed.

"We must free him." Constance had an idea. "We must kill the thicket, in a natural way."

"With cold!" Velo came up with the idea.

"Yes, freeze it," Verity enjoined.

"By golly, yes." Constance prepared for enchantment. "Cold brings death to all that was green. Frozen weather forces living back to ground. Winds of winter come right now, make yourself seen. Put rest the bramble and bring white peace around."

A gentle cool breeze released a few flurries. Suddenly, white flakes filled the skies. Within moments winter embraced the land. Mounds of snow and ice covered every inch of New London.

The Fae found Phillip's armaments and brought them to the Prince. He was shivering as they struck the thorny shrubs away with his sword and shield. With the bitter cold, the thicket broke into blackened pieces and fell against the brilliant snow.

"Hurry to the Princess!" Velo cried out over the blowing wind.

"Yes, to Rose!" Verity urged and helped Phillip to the ground.

"Wait!" Constance warned. Out of the corner of her eye she saw an enormous dark beast coming.

It was a brass mechanical dragon that was almost as tall as the palace. Its laser green eyes beamed into the snow and melted it. It approached with heavy steps that shook the ground around them. When it reached the collapsing briars, the dragon paused, opened its mouth, and shot blistering flames at the good Fae.

"Yikes!" Velo screamed.

"Oh, my goodness." Verity flew out of the path of the burn.

"Prince Phillip! You must stop it," Constance called.

The mechanical legs squealed and groaned as the robotic beast lumbered forward. With a swing of its tail, it lashed at the palace and caused part of the wall to crumble.

The Prince whistled for Maverick as he gathered his sword and shield. The Fae flew to his side.

"You have the sword of truth," Velo gushed.

"And the shield of virtue," Verity panted.

"You have the tools to halt it. It is not within our powers to stop mechanical things." Constance looked carefully at the dragon as it prepared to strike again. "Perhaps stop the fire?"

"Yes, yes! That's it!" Prince Phillip jumped on Maverick and rode directly in front of the mighty mechanical dragon. "Virtue wins over all!" he yelled as he threw his sword as hard as he could right into the mouth of the beast. The weapon spliced the fuel lines and ruptured the electricity to its eyes. The dragon fell silent as steam shot from its vents.

Prince Phillip and the Fae backed away. "It's going to explode! Take cover." He pulled the Fae under his coat and throttled Maverick to the other side of the castle.

With an intense roar, the dragon crumpled to its knees and belched a column of angry red and black smoke. Hinges of a door on its underside creaked as Malena crawled out.

"There's no time, you must get to the Princess." Velo tugged at the Prince.

"Yes to Rose." Verity popped out from under his riding coat.

"You must save the kingdom." Constance charged ahead. "Come!"

"Did you say Rose? Rose is the Princess?" Prince Phillip grinned.

"Yes!" the Fae chimed.

They rode into the palace with Maverick's metal hooves clattering over the elegant marble. Once inside, they were aghast at the staff and subjects stumbling about in an odd daze.

"Her bedroom is that way!" Constance clung to the Prince's top hat as they stomped up the carpeted steps and into the living quarters of the royals.

Phillip reared Maverick up and knocked down the bedroom door with a thud. He dismounted in a hurry and ran to Rose's bedside.

"It's her, really her. But is she dead?" he questioned the Fae.

"No, just asleep." Velo smiled.

"Yes, asleep. Cursed to sleep, almost to death by Malena." Verity grinned.

"Until awakened by a true love's kiss." Constance waved at Rose. "Go on now! It's you, Sir. No need to be too gentlemanly. Kiss her!"

And with that encouragement, the Prince leaned in and placed a delicate, lovely kiss on the lips of his betrothed.

"Mmmm." Rose's eyes fluttered as she awoke.

"Rose?"

"Prince Phillip?"

"Yes! It's me. You're safe." He touched her serene face with a gentle hand.

"In the wood?"

"No, we're in the palace." He helped her up.

"The spell has been broken." Velo glowed.

"You won't need protection." Verity glimmered.

"All is well!" Constance gleamed.

Noises of the castle's inhabitants awakening echoed through the building. Soon the royals were reunited and the sounds of happy cheers filled the kingdom.

The cooks started to prepare breakfast. Housekeepers and maids cleaned the halls and lit the gas lamps. The groundskeepers gathered the remains of the once terrifying briars and collected them for firewood. It would soon be time to celebrate a birthday and a royal wedding.

"Well done. Splendid!" King Stephen slapped the shoulder of his future son-in-law.

The Prince shook his hand and then embraced his bride-to-be. "Happy Birthday!" He again kissed Rose and the Fae flitted around them in a joyous dance.

"So all is settled. We should rest a while. Morning will be here soon enough." Queen Layla tugged at the King's hand.

"Wait," Rose cried. "May I speak with Papa alone?"

"Of course, of course." Queen Layla led the Prince and the Fae outside the parlor.

"What is it, my dear?" the King inquired.

"There is so much here, almost too much. I mean things. Equipment. I mean, items that aren't of nature. I know that progress can't be stopped, but can't we preserve what we have?" Rose implored her father.

"I have an idea. Stay here, I will speak with the Fae. I will see you at breakfast." He kissed the forehead of his daughter. She was absolutely right.

—

Malena stumbled into the cold snow absolutely defeated. The bitter cold stung her skin as she prepared to die. A familiar voice came from behind. "Malena."

"Let me die in peace you fool!" she hissed. Small, weak tendrils of smoke eased from her horns. The nubs of her wings ached, for in the destructive blast of the dragon, her artificial wings were torn away.

"Malena. You were wronged." King Stephen came forward in the dim light of the sunrise. The Fae came from behind him and alighted near the fallen sorceress. "The anger of a few has tormented many. I do not wish you death, although you had cursed my child to die. Your forest was taken without proper consideration for nature. I am wise enough to see the jealousy of my Queen and the effect of modern times on our environment. The Princess Aurore has enlightened me further of my faults. I have authorized the Fae to return you to your wood if you agree to remain there and protect it from all others. You won't be able to leave it, but it will be sacred and no modern machinery will ever enter it. Can you agree to these terms?" The King knelt at Malena's side.

"Yes," the sorceress whispered in agony.

"Very well then." Velo grasped her wand.

"Yes, it is to be done." Verity locked arms with her sisters.

"Ahem." Constance prepared their spell. The Fae united their wands. "So then anger buried and turned to rust, a return to the permanent wood, Malena must. To remain there ever so shall she protect, and from the harm of material progress, ever deflect." With a puff of pastel smoke, Malena disappeared.

Just then, dawn broke over New London as the skies seemed to clear of smog and the choke of pollution. People in the city and villages marveled at the blue skies and pristine white clouds that glowed with the sunrise. The remaining snow conjured by the Fae melted away.

Rose stood with Prince Phillip at the door of the palace. "Ah, sunrise. An awakening. Good morning, my Princess Rose."

"It's Aurore. I'm named for the dawn." She smiled as he leaned in for a tender kiss.

In the days since then, the trees and shrubbery exploded with greenery so quickly that the groundskeepers could barely keep them properly groomed. Butterflies and bees tickled the new flowers in the city's grand gardens. At night, the fireflies danced with the Fae.

A decree was spread throughout the land that no one would be allowed to hunt or partake of the far green wood, and anyone who should break such law would be at the mercy of its protector. Peace reigned with progress, and all lived happily ever after.

Odyssey?

by Aaron Isett

He had gotten them this far. They had lived through the Crimea, in spite of the best efforts of the Russians and the bloody incompetence of the brass. The company had even made it to Istanbul for resupply and recreation. Of course, not everyone had made it. But the ones that had survived the Russians and the cold and the weather and the flu and the water... They had made it this far, and he would be damned if ouzo and women would get them all killed now! At least, Captain Ulysses Thrakoniso of Her Majesty's Royal Marines was determined that it wouldn't.

That was why he was briskly slapping his men out of their drunken stupors. Most of the company was back at the dockside quarters they had procured. Some of his junior officers had accompanied him to indulge in the things that made fighting a war worth the privations they had endured. Fortunately, all had enjoyed their vices with relative dignity. Unfortunately, a few of those vices, who had indulged in the Marines equally enthusiastically, were now at the door, trying to hold back several angry men who looked like they might be related.

It would certainly not do to be caught of a morning brawling in a place like this, especially since they had a ship to catch. The dawn light hurt his eyes as Ulysses, Lieutenant Lamb, and Sergeants Stern and Morgan all fumbled into wakefulness and headed for the back door, Lamb snatching the last of the ouzo as they went,. He poured the last of it into his mouth with a grimace. Hair of the dog, but what a dog it was. Torrents of curses in Turkish that undoubtedly accused them of being descendants of some variety of animal followed them as the men made their way into the place, knocking the furniture aside with crashes and bangs. "That's our cue to leave, gents", Ulysses called, slamming the door behind them. It was just a matter of a hard run to the docks and up to the ship, the… What was it… The HMS Sable.

The autonomous crew had finished loading the last of the mens' belongings onto the ship not long before. The only ones not aboard were themselves, and they were approaching rapidly. Their boots thundered up the gangplank, though their haste wasn't strictly necessary at that point, having lost, or at least delayed, their pursuit sufficiently to get aboard safely. As they stopped and caught their breath, Ulysses grinned at them, looking like proper wrecks.

"Alright, mum's the word, gents, but let's get a quick wash and shave. Then, turn the troops out for inspection. We'll be departing–" Here he was interrupted by the ship's horn. "Now, it seems. See to it."

Wonderfully efficient, these new troop ships, even if the brassy automatons that crewed them gave him the heebie-jeebies sometimes. He went below decks to his officer's cabin, a privilege that was almost jarring to him after the hardships of the Crimea. There was a basin with a mirror over it and water, a comfortable bed, and even a small writing desk for dispatches and letters home. Once he was cleaned up, he polished his boots and gave a shout to Lieutenant Lamb. The men were all assembled on deck posthaste as the brassy crew worked around them.

"Men, we're on our way home from a tour of the Crimea I shouldn't care to take again. We're one of the lucky companies to be on one of the new automated troop transports. So we can just

26

relax, right?!" No one said anything. They knew better. "Wrong. We are still Royal Marines and will comport ourselves as such. Which means that if there is work to do that the machines do not, we shall. And we shall also ensure that we are fit and turned out in readiness for duty." He could feel the temper of the men sour a bit. "That said, this will be an easy journey. So long as we don't get sloppy, we're well-provisioned with good food, lots of fresh water, and enough comforts to last us twice the journey, if we needed it." That cheered the men up considerably. "Now, as our leave in Istanbul was short, I'm extending it by a day. Relax here on ship, let the machines do the job, and do not interfere with them. Dismissed!"

Captain Thrakoniso then put himself at the highest vantage point on the ship that was shaded from the noonday sun and sat, watching the marvelous mechanical crew as they labored with keeping the craft shipshape. It was fascinating to watch. Lieutenant Lamb joined him, a jug of water in one hand, a bottle of wine in the other.

"Look at them work away, Captain," remarked Lamb, gesturing to the automatons at their labors below. "How long until they make ones that can fight, and just replace us altogether, eh?"

"And what would war mean then, Lieutenant? When generals can just send the machines to do it and count the cost in scrap metal and labor costs? When it means nothing to die for a cause and even less to kill for it? When the people we fight face only a faceless army of brass men, are we no better than demons?" the Captain mused. Then he thought of all the men he had lost, all the men he had seen ordered into the meat grinder of grape shot and musket balls, dying in droves as a sacrifice to the pride of second and third sons whose fathers had bought their commissions. Maybe fighting wars with machines would be less terrible than he supposed.

They continued their philosophizing and debating, as they had the whole way through the cold, muddy, bloody hell that was the Crimea, until the sun set, and soon they, and the men, all tucked in to a meal and went, some slowly and some more quickly, to sleep.

—

That night, the Captain's sleep was disturbed, or at least accompanied by, the strange and wonderful sound of song. It was the song heard at the edge of hearing, beyond comprehension of lyric, barely enough for melody or rhythm to catch the ear, yet irresistible nonetheless. When the Captain managed to shake his head awake and free of the song, he almost missed it, whatever tune it was. Once he fell again asleep, the rest of his dreams were the song of booted feet and cannon fire.

He awoke early. Even earlier than had become his habit as a Marine and an officer. He was washed, shaved, dressed, and on deck before the first light crept over the horizon to another gorgeous, Mediterranean blue day. He ascended the wheelhouse, hand sliding over the worn, smooth railing that so many had touched before. When he reached the deck near the wheel, manned by the unnervingly silent brass helmsman, he turned and went aft, looking out at the startlingly clear azure water. He took a deep breath of the salt air and smelled... oranges?

"Couldn't sleep, either, Captain?"

"It is rather early, isn't it?" Ulysses replied, not allowing Sergeant Stern the luxury of thinking he had caught him off guard. The big Londoner was surprisingly quiet for his size.

"Even for you, Captain," Stern agreed. Ulysses took the orange slices that the Sergeant offered. "I heard something about the waters we'll be sailing through, Captain." Stern leaned against the guard rail, deliberately casual.

"Something from the local rumor mill, Sergeant?" Ulysses inquired with a smile, knowing that, despite not making an effort, the Sergeant would always have the best local gossip. The man was a natural information gatherer, speaking several languages. When he was asked why he did not work with the scouts or intelligence services, Stern always replied that he hated lying. This was accompanied by a look so fierce that no one ever followed it up, except for the Captain.

"Aye, Captain. Local legends put us right in the waters where uncharted islands appear and disappear with the summer storms. They say that beasts and monsters reside there that few men see and live to tell the tale. Tales tell of Sirens that can lure ships to wreck with song." The Sergeant looked genuinely uncomfortable.

"That sounds like something out of a child's storybook, Sergeant," Ulysses answered, finishing off the orange slices.

"What, like metal men sailing a craft through the sea, Captain?" Stern replied, a smirk crossing his face.

"...Thank you for volunteering to lead drills this morning," The Captain acknowledged with a chuckle. He knew that his subordinate had won that exchange, but that was the nice thing about authority. He didn't have to be right to be right.

That was not to say that he failed to participate. In fact, he, Lieutenant Lamb, and Sergeant Morgan were on the forecastle, fencing and wrestling all morning, the sun quickly warming them as it rose into the sky, burning mercilessly, reddening many of the lads and browning others.

After taking a particularly rough toss from the Captain, Lamb shook his head. "In this heat, going like this, how are you still fresh as a daisy, Captain?" As he helped him up, Ulysses leaned down and whispered in Lamb's ear.

"My first rule of leading men. You can let them see you sweat, you let them see you struggle, but you make sure they see you win." He marched to the wheelhouse, bare chested and sweating, and dismissed the men. He got cleaned up in his cabin, then put on the uniform. Time for another day.

One problem, he mused, with having a mechanical crew for the ship, was that he had no ship's captain or navigator to pester with questions, nor did he have any such crew from whom he could learn more sailing skills. Ulysses satisfied his instinct to be productive with dividing the Marines into work shifts. Upkeep of the ship was still important, and there were tasks that the clockwork crew could not do, at least not safely. That would also ensure that the men were occupied instead of getting bored and restless. Idle hands and all that, like his grandfather had told him.

—

Things continued like this for a few days before disaster struck. The evening meal was finished, and the men had retired, except for the night watch. The day had been the usual blue skies and blue water, but a shout from the lookout had Ulysses up on deck in a trice. It was like they were in another sea, just another day on the Mediterranean. By the time he had gotten topside, the wind had picked up considerably, and it was far darker than the previous nights. He couldn't figure out why until he realized that the brilliant stars and the moon were no longer visible. The deck began pitching to an alarming degree, and he had to grab hold of the railing by the wheelhouse stairs to avoid sprawling along the boards.

Ulysses immediately barked down into the galley: "ALL HANDS ON DECK!"

His command was quickly relayed and every man of the company was busy at work, readying the ship to survive the storm. The more they worked, the worse the storm got. The hours wore on until the Captain realized that, hardy as they were, there would be an accident if he and the men kept pushing to keep the ship sailing. That was when he gave the order.

"Batten it down! We have to ride this out!"

The ship's company headed below decks for some well-deserved rest, clothes soaked to the skin, many with bruises or rope burns, but none seriously harmed.

Ulysses pulled Lamb, Stern, and Morgan aside. "We have to make sure that the ship is seaworthy through the night and in the morning. The four of us can split a night shift in my cabin, one man in the wheelhouse." He could tell he was about to get objections. "We're responsible for these men. No arguments. Besides, I have coffee and rum in my cabin." That mollified the men somewhat.

The night passed slowly, helped along by the copious amounts of coffee and not-quite-so-copious amounts of rum involved. The Captain pulled the last shift, just before dawn. The storm was horrible, and the rest of the men had passed out around his cabin or their own. As the captain drank down the last of his coffee and stood to head up to the deck, he heard a terrific bang, like a battery of cannon going off at once, but sharper.

He rushed on deck, barely pausing to don his oilskins, boots slipping on a deck slick with rain. He peered through the rain, and was aghast at what he saw. The brass crewmen who had manned the helm and navigational instruments, which had been preset for their heading of Gibraltar, were gone. Well, not gone. There were a pair of smoking wrecks, piles of brass plating, gears, and crystals lying near where the two were stationed. There was no fire, nor any damage to the wheel or instruments, so far as he could tell, but there was no one to hold the helm. So that's what he did. He held them on course as best he could, according to the compass, which almost certainly did not stay level for any length of time. His hands slipped and slid on the wheel, but he held it tight, until his forearms burned and he had to grit his teeth and growl against the wind and rain. He had no idea how long he stood there, trying to keep their course steady, for he knew they were being driven before the storm.

—

Morning dawned, as it always had, and always would. This one was dreary and gray, though the rain had stopped. The waves and wind were all calmer. Captain Ulysses Thrakoniso stood at the wheel to greet the sun. When the men clambered up the ladders from the hold, they saw the metal crew unclamping themselves from the ship's furniture and smokestack. That must have been the emergency protocol for heavy weather, Ulysses realized. After all, it wasn't as if the bloody things could swim. While the men gaped around at the disorder that the ship was in after the storm, the Captain tossed off his oilskins and straightened out his uniform. Though it would never have passed parade ground inspection, it looked better than it had any right to, given the circumstances.

"Don't just stand there gawking, men! Attention! You're

still Marines, aren't you?!" the Captain barked. They assembled smartly at attention. "As you can see, the ship is in disarray following last night's bit of weather. Morgan, Stern, you're in charge of dividing work details to inspect this whole ship. I want reports of the damage, what can be repaired, and the supplies we need to do it, as well as an inventory of the stores and supplies, if anything was ruined. You know the drill." He nodded to the company cook. "Hall, brew coffee for everyone. We will need to be awake for this. Lamb, you're with me. Dismissed!"

The Captain and Lieutenant Lamb spent the next few hours drinking coffee, checking the compass, sextant, and other instruments, and trying to figure out where they had been blown. The bad news just got worse when Morgan came to the wheelhouse.

"Captain. Our rudder has been damaged. It's swinging a bit loose from the housing," he told Ulysses as the Captain sipped some coffee. Ulysses paused, setting his mug down slowly to show that he was unconcerned. That, and to prevent himself from throwing the mug across the deck.

"Can we fix it, Morgan?" he asked. The Sergeant was the most experienced carpenter he knew in the company, so he would be the man to know.

"That depends on how the tools and supplies look, sir. I will see what I can do when Sergeant Stern is done with the inventory and inspection," Morgan told him.

Ulysses' face was still impassive, but the men in the cabin could see that he was all steel, standing on will alone after the storm.

"Make it good, Sergeant. We're already off course, and we can ill afford to be further off. Understood?" he replied. The Sergeant's salute had enough snap to express his affirmative. "Very good, Sergeant."

At the end of a full day of hard, sweaty work, the Captain addressed the men. "Last night's storm robbed us of our navigator and steersman, as well as blowing us well off course. The repairs you made today will prove to be vital in correcting our position and heading, and ensuring that we get home. Good work today, men. Extra rum all around, and get some sleep. We will all need it."

Once they had done what they could to plot a position for the Sable, Ulysses retired to his cabin and fell into his bunk like a stone and slept like the dead. And yet, when he woke up, he could hear a faint snatch of song.

—

The next week was spent steaming in the straightest line possible, catching strange fish to stretch their food supplies, and desperately, feverishly, attempting to plot their course against the navigational charts and aids they had on board. At least the fishing gave some entertainment, and variety, in their diet. Citrus kept the scurvy away, but it was a poor substitute for novel flavors.

The Captain felt like he never slept a wink. His dreams, as usual, were plagued by restless visions of the past. Blood, the shouts of men, and the screams of horses filled his nightmares. The only respite was the song. By now, the Captain could almost hear the music in the daytime. He always had it halfway on his mind. He had to remind himself frequently that it was the safe return of himself and his men home he was concerned about.

One unusually foggy evening, well after the meal was finished, the Captain pulled another shift at the wheel. The lookout called, "Land ho, Captain!"

Ulysses had not been himself all day. The song had lingered too long in his head. He pulled Lieutenant Lamb and Sergeant Morgan aside. "I need you to obey this order in strictest confidence. Pull all the men except for the automatons below. I want you to lash me to the bowsprit and rails, fastly so I cannot move, and plug your ears so you can hear nothing. Then, guide us around the shoals near the island." When Lamb made to argue, a fierce scowl silenced him. "I need to hear it, Lamb. It sounds like… forgiveness."

Morgan knew exactly what the Captain meant, though he hardly seemed able to believe it himself. It was a testament to

Ulysses' leadership, or their credulity, that they obeyed him without question.

—

When the Lieutenant freed the Captain from his bounds a few hours of sailing later, Ulysses Thrakoniso looked changed. He had a look on his face like a recruit who had just seen battle for the first time, but instead of the horror and mud and blood and din of the carnal struggles that had been their bread and butter, it was something so beautiful it brought tears to the hard man's eyes.

The Captain stood, just for a moment, lost in thought. Then he turned to Lamb and Morgan, and did something neither of them ever thought he would do. He could have punched them, bawled them out, or thrown them over the side, and they would have been less surprised than when he reached out and hugged them tight, just for a long moment.

When he straightened up again, it was as if the weight of the universe had been lifted from his shoulders. "Now let's go home," he said.

—

If you asked them what changed about him, they could never really say. They might think, sometimes, that he was less angry, but they would correct themselves remembering an incident wherein his anger saved them from a gruesome fate. They might say he was more circumspect, but then recall that his decisiveness in the face of the odds made them love him. No, what changed, they decided, was that they never again saw him sleepless and restless. You might ask them what was in the song, and perhaps it is different for each listener. But for the Captain, they might tell you, it was some kind of peace.

The Marionette

by Phoebe Darqueling

You will no doubt think me mad. For though this is a confession, it is not a confession to the crime that has brought me to this cell. Of that, I am innocent, or if not wholly innocent, I can say that no blood was spilled by my hand. My sins run far deeper than a simple murder, and I confess them now, not in the hopes of unburdening my soul (Heaven's gates are surely closed to the likes of me), but to deter others from ever repeating Geppetto's terrible experiment.

When this all started, I had already been an apprentice to the clockmaker for several years. I had in fact surpassed my Maestro by this time and worked on projects his tired old eyes could no longer handle. Geppetto mostly carved and polished the wooden bodies of the clocks while I did the more delicate work of shaping and installing the mechanisms. He was fond of telling me that I was more than just his ward, that he regarded me as a son. And so, I stayed long after I could have made my own way in the world. Perhaps this is why he brought me into his confidence, or perhaps he simply needed my nimble fingers and unclouded eyes to build what he could not.

Along with an old gray cat, we lived in private rooms adjoining the workshop. I knew some of what he did with his time outside of the working hours. He often came home on Saturdays with a folio of pages or a scroll under his arm. On these nights, he would take his supper into his room and not emerge until morning, or a few times he remained there for several days. On the rare occasion his door was left ajar, I had seen an array of beakers and pouches full of bright liquids and powders, and the faint scent of rotten eggs permeated the air. I even once glimpsed the ornately adorned documents. The images were beautifully and, dare I say, lovingly rendered, if occasionally grotesque.

At the time, I had assumed from the many colors of his materials that he was trying to duplicate these strange pictures, illuminating his own versions with brush and pigment. In a way, I suppose he was, but not in the manner I had surmised.

I did not learn the truth until I completed the cricket. While Geppetto spent his free hours poring over the documents in the privacy of his chamber, I worked on my own mechanical projects in mine. Though it took many a painstaking evening, I eventually built a functioning clockwork insect. By necessity, it was larger than a real cricket, but still fit in the palm of my hand. I proudly showed the Maestro how it would hop, then, just as the real animal, it would rub its wings together to chirp twice before hopping again. This rhythm is what earned it the name "Giacomo." One had to be vigilant to keep my dear Giacomo from jumping right off the table edge, but at the risk of boasting, it was a rather fine mechanism.

I had expected my Maestro to be delighted, but was surprised (and I will admit, rather disheartened) to see his face grow serious and thoughtful upon my presentation. I remember worrying that he was displeased that I had used valuable materials on such an enterprise and without his permission. I was mumbling my way through an apology when he rose from the table and rushed to his room. He returned immediately, something clutched in his hand but hidden from view.

Geppetto asked me then what I knew of transmutation.

The realm of the spiritual had never held much sway for me. It had never really occurred to me that my mentor had any sort of philosophical tendencies himself, but he laid out the principle of ascension, both spiritually and physically, of a lowly substance to something grander. I recall to this day the way his eyes seemed to glow with a sort of madness as he spoke, and I am ashamed to admit that I found myself catching his fever.

As I learned that day and in those to come, transmutation could be achieved through the use of a substance called the Philosopher's Stone. The early alchemists had been primarily concerned with changing one metal to another or ingesting the Philosopher's Stone, which could prolong their lives. Still others viewed alchemy as a means to bring a soul to new heights, unlocking one's greatest potential through refinement the way the first alchemists refined chemicals. Geppetto believed these different aspects were not exclusive, but part of the same line of thought. Like a coin, each of these faces were intertwined, and while the stone could not prolong or enrich human life, it could give an organic substance a chance to transcend its bounds. In short, to grant metal creations the gift of life.

As impressive as Giacomo was already, the Maestro insisted that he had the power to give it a will of its own. That is when he opened his palm and revealed its contents. A tiny wooden box rested there, finely carved and covered with a beautifully wrought inlay of brass. His hands shook with excitement as he undid the clasp, and he steadied his breath before opening it. Inside there was no more than a spoonful a fine red powder with amber flecks glinting in the candlelight.

I was skeptical of his claims (as any reasonable man would be) and was shocked when he then asked for permission to apply this strange concoction to my cricket. Apparently, he had tried it out on some mundane clockwork and believed the mechanism had communicated with him by dint of refusing to turn the hands any longer. This sounded to me very much like he had simply broken it. I did not like the idea of the careful cleaning it would take to rid my dear Giacomo's gears of the substance later, but Geppetto seemed so earnest and excited, I found I could not deny him the opportunity. With the aid of soft brush, he gently dusted the entire cricket with his russet powder inside and out.

He sent me to make our breakfast as he worked, and I worried all the while that my lovely insect would never be the same after his attentions. In my mind, I began to work out my next design, on ways to improve on the next model when Giacomo was inevitably ruined. So lost in thought was I that it took me some minutes before I realized I could hear chirping behind me. Not two chirps as I had built the cricket to make, but a continuous and merry song.

When I returned to the table, Geppetto was crooning gently and stroking the clockwork insect's antennae. Giacomo turned its head to watch me as I took my seat, then took two purposeful hops in my direction. The Maestro's milky eyes were wide with wonder, and I felt a giggle bubble up from somewhere inside of me as the cricket delicately nudged my finger with its head. I cannot say for certain how long we sat there together marveling over this thing we had created together, but sometime after night came, we began to speak of what else we could build and bestow with life.

That is when, God forgive me, we decided to build the marionette.

—

It took me several weeks to tool each gear and work out how to connect the levers and pulleys to its limbs, but they passed in a blur of excitement. Giacomo kept me company at my bench. We worked out a simple system of communication; one chirp for yes, two chirps for no. Whether because it was made of metal or because it was made by my hand, the cricket seemed to possess a deep understanding of the work I was doing and endeavored to aid me when possible. I had worried at first that the cat would mistake Giacomo for a morsel or plaything, but the animal actually seemed to avoid my lovely cricket as much as possible. I was glad of it then, but I cannot help but wonder now if the old ratter could somehow sense the wrongness of this artificial being.

During this time, Geppetto set to work on the other parts of our project. We agreed that it should have a body made of wood to avoid any chance that the limbs would be too heavy for it to lift. After all, this marionette would have no strings to aid its movements, only my clockwork heart and Geppetto's marvelous powder. This first effort was modest, just simple pine wood shaped with care to make up the body. When he did not know I was looking, I often saw the old man clutch the puppet to his chest and whisper promises in a low and loving voice to the pinewood boy.

This little "pinocchio" was to be just the beginning; someday we would make our creatures from mahogany and silver. Over the dinner hour we would discuss how we would tour the world with our beautiful creation and how people would shower us with their affection and, of course, their gold. Over breakfasts we talked of a whole troupe of puppets capable of acting out scenes of great comedy and drama for the royal courts of Europe. Soon, in our minds we were already rich and powerful men with the world at our fingertips.

By far, the most difficult part to render was the face. I wanted to do something simple for the first model, but Geppetto insisted that even this first attempt at a marionette must be able to speak. Giacomo's simple chirping would not satisfy the Maestro, he wanted our boy to be able to express himself. I took apart a music box to give it a way to make different tones and installed a moveable jaw. Then came the demand for eyes that could swivel, so I rigged up a special shaft and hinge to give the puppet's painted eyes some range of movement. I drew the line at blinking, for a wooden eyeball would never need to be moistened.

As I completed the mechanical parts of the marionette, my mentor also went to work to generate more of the Philosopher's Stone to ensure we had enough to coat the entire puppet when it was finished. The process was arduous and required several different stages of mutation, or so he said. As close as this great project brought us together, the Maestro would not allow me to see how he created it. This bothered me a little at the time, but now I am glad that I do not know the terrible secret and others cannot extract it from me.

Even knowing what I know now, I think of that time fondly. It may have even been the best of my life. Then in a flash came the fateful day – it was time for Pinocchio to wake.

—

As Geppetto went to work on the marionette with his brush and his powder, he sent me to the market to fetch a fine bottle of wine. He assured me that we would be celebrating before the sun went down. As I walked the streets of my beloved Firenze that day, I remember grinning so wide my friends and even strangers stopped me to ask what had made me so happy. Many assumed some comely maiden put the spring in my step, others saw the wine in my hand and thought I was besotted. I answered their entreaties in riddles, enjoying the looks of puzzlement on their faces almost as much as I reveled in my anticipated joy of success. By the time I returned to the workshop, I felt as if my heart would burst, and my cheeks burned from all of the smiling. I was a fool.

When I entered the workshop again, it felt as though a cloud had blotted out the sun. The Maestro sat perfectly still, elbows propped on the table and face buried in his hands. Pinocchio lay motionless on the table next to a completely empty powder box. Even in the meager light I could see the dusting of red all over his body even thicker than the coat Geppetto had applied to my cricket. I stood in the doorway for a long minute before I had the courage to enter and make my presence known.

Upon seeing me, my mentor flew into a violent rage. He stood so quickly that he knocked the bench over and immediately rounded the table, arms outstretched as if he would strangle me. My shock rendered me as still and unyielding as the marionette as he shouted himself to tears. He accused me of sabotaging the device, of being an ungrateful and lazy boy. He ranted that I had done my best work on my own creation while shirking my responsibility to him. Every time I thought I would be able to speak, he found a new way to do injury with his brutal words until he had thoroughly exhausted himself. Once he finally sank onto the floor to weep, I placed the bottle on the table and made my way to my room.

I only allowed myself a few moments of sulking before I pulled out my schematics. I knew I had done everything perfectly; there was no reason for the marionette to lie there like the lifeless dolls it resembled. Geppetto's sobbing lasted for some time, but thankfully he did not come to my door. My shock had subsided and was becoming a low-burning anger at the unfairness of his words, and I feared what I might say to the old man if he came at me again. Eventually, the house was silent but for the occasional inquiring chirp from my clockwork cricket, proof that the Philosopher's Stone worked even if Pinocchio lay still.

In time, I grew tired of looking over the plans I already knew were flawless and lay down to rest. When I woke, I realized the fault had to be in the powder and hoped that the Maestro would have come to the same conclusion by the time I saw him. I opened my door a crack, though when I peered out there was no sign of my mentor. It was far past the normal time for Geppetto to be abed, but I supposed it had been a very hard night for the both of us. I stretched and staggered into the kitchen to light the morning fire and start the porridge.

The marionette remained as we had left it, unblinking eyes staring forlornly at the ceiling. The bottle, however, was gone and more than likely the wine with it. I took the opportunity to look the puppet over in private, but all seemed in order. Upon opening the hatch in the chest, I could see the rust-colored powder coating every pin, every cog. I tested the winding mechanism, the springs, and all were as they should be. All the while, those eerie blue eyes bore into me and I found myself with the sudden urge to put distance between myself and puppet before Geppetto came out looking for the breakfast that I hadn't even started making. I set the marionette on a chair near the fireplace and went about my usual morning tasks.

I started a pot of water boiling, then swept the floors. As I made my way around the workshop, I felt my gaze inexorably drawn back to Pinocchio. It continued to slump in the chair, one arm dangling over the side at an odd angle. The unnatural posture only reinforced how artificial the little body was, how far from a living, breathing being the marionette was despite its carved human features. Yet I continued to glimpse over my shoulder, a part of me certain that I sensed some kind of intelligence in its fixed gaze.

I completed my chores and broke my fast (careful to take a seat that did not put my back to those painted eyes), but Geppetto still did not emerge. No doubt the wine and woe were competing to keep him beneath the covers. A part of me hoped he would stay there all day, while the other seethed at his sloth. All of the shame he had heaped on me the night before for his failings were turning to a bitterness and rage. I am usually a tender-hearted fellow, and I usually simply forgave and forgot my mentor's flares of temper once I had received an apology. But the longer he hid behind that door, the greater my resentment grew.

I sat at the table for some time, lost in my own thoughts as I composed cutting rebukes to the prior evening's accusations. At some point, the cat leaped onto the table to investigate my cooling gruel, startling me out of my reverie. My eyes fell once again to Pinocchio. The tongues of flame cast shifting light and shadows across the marionette, and I contented myself that this was the source of my earlier unease. It would be easy to mistake the dance of light for movement. I scolded myself for my childishness and left my half-eaten breakfast on the table, giving the silly beast a gentle scratch under the chin to show my gratitude for bringing me out of my dark thoughts.

I believed then, as I do now, that the best remedy for any unpleasant feelings – be they a bout of nerves or the petulance I felt for the Maestro – is to focus on a task. Our failed enterprise had consumed our waking hours for weeks, and there was paying work that needed doing if we were to continue to eat. I checked our records to find a suitable project, then crossed to my work bench. As had become my habit, I talked to Giacomo, laying out the steps I was about to take for my little assistant. As I spoke, it was as if lead gathered in my stomach for I realized I had not heard the cricket's chirping since the previous night. By the time my eyes fell on the assortment of metallic scrap that had once been my finest achievement (and I will admit, a dear friend) I felt so heavy with worry, I thought I might fall straight through the floor.

The cricket's legs splayed out from its nearly flattened body, which had no doubt been crushed by the hammer resting nearby. In a single, merciless blow, the assailant had utterly destroyed the poor creature. I remember standing there gawking for several seconds, then my rage flashed bright and red before my eyes. The wretch Geppetto had to be behind it, his jealousy over my skill and the knowledge of his own failings must have driven him to lash out – or so I believed.

Before I even realized what I was doing, I had stalked over to the Maestro's chamber door and thrown it wide. Without preamble, I started shouting at him for all manner of sins. I do not recall everything I said, though I do know some of it was unwarranted. I could forgive him for his show of passion when he had wrongly admonished me the previous night. But there was something so cruel and terrible about the notion that he had crushed Giacomo that I gave way to my passion.

Just as I had suspected, Geppetto clutched the empty bottle to him. When the door struck the wall, the sound woke him with a start, and it fell to the packed earth of the floor. I do not remember when I picked it up, or when I began to wave it threateningly at him, so blinded was I with my rage. My voice undoubtedly carrying through the neighborhood as I railed at the old man. It was only when I saw how he cowered that I even noticed I held the bottle in my hand. He made no attempt to deny the murder of Giacomo, and as I took stock of myself and the fear in his eyes, the anger drained from me as quickly as it had come. Imagine my shame, to see him looking at me like I was a crazed animal. I fell to my knees, and bringing his hand to my lips, I begged for his forgiveness.

So engrossed was I that I almost didn't notice the tinkling chime coming from the workshop, as if a music box had somehow been taught to laugh. If only I had known then what I know now, I could have ended the horror right then and there. Instead, it proved to be only the beginning.

—

To his credit, the Maestro never mentioned the incident again. He was likely as embarrassed by his own outburst as I had been by mine, and we both seemed content not to address it. I wish now that I had pressed him for a confession, which may have helped us to understand what had occurred sooner.

The marionette remained on its perch near the fireplace, but we did not speak of it or our failure for several days. Whether it was because I grew accustomed to its presence or my shame kept me from glancing toward the spot, I lost my awareness of the clockwork boy. Geppetto and I kept ourselves busy catching up on the commissions, he with his stains and paints and I with my brass and steel.

When Geppetto let out a cry three days later, it was the first I had thought of Pinocchio at all. I was startled by the sound and rushed to my mentor's side. The cat had apparently taken interest in the dangling arm and the Maestro shooed it away. And so we found ourselves standing shoulder to shoulder over the marionette. He blushed at the strength of his reaction, and as it sometimes happens, the tension between us gave way to a bout of laughter. The strain of the past few days suddenly snapped like a string, and we were soon clapping each other on the shoulder with affection. This light mood soon had us talking again of our imagined future with our band of puppets, and we both agreed to comb over our separate pieces of the project for some hint at what had gone wrong. We spoke no more of blame, only of how we both wished to see success. So, with renewed vigor, I brought Pinocchio to my table and Geppetto disappeared once again into his room to create more of the Philosopher's Stone.

I pored over an anatomy book and checked every

articulated finger, every lever and pulley that would allow it to move its limbs. I replaced the leather straps with the durability and flexibility of rubber to better emulate the tendons of the human body. I adjusted the clockwork innards with delicate care, though my tools seemed to jump from my hand at times. Though I was quick to blame my own excitement, over time I realized the mechanism itself was prone to jerking. I spent hours tightening and loosening various springs, thinking it was some flaw in my design or the parts I had so painstakingly crafted.

When I brought the problem before the Maestro, he made the pronouncement that I must be tickling the poor boy, and I should be more careful. The words were said in jest, but reflected the feeling growing within us both that we had created something more than just a mere toy. The more time and attention we lavished on Pinocchio, the more often Geppetto referred to the thing as a "he" rather than an "it."

The Maestro returned to his habit of talking to the marionette in the evenings, and even read out loud to the thing on occasion. Though I did not share his level of affection, I did not begrudge the old man his attachment. Unmarried and childless as he was, he no doubt felt some need to fulfill a paternal longing through his attentions, and as long as he held the key to the alchemical processes necessary to manufacture the stone, we needed one another to get past our earlier failure. Through our intellect and hard work, we would water the fertile soil of the public's imaginations, and once we had our living dolls, we were certain gold would spring from it like wildflowers.

It was not until I found the blood that I came to suspect that we had never failed at all.

—

I was woken from sleep one night by the most awful sound. In my stupor, I did not at first recognize the screech as coming from inside the house. When I heard the second yowl and the crash of tools in the workshop, I sprang from my bed and rushed to see to the matter. The Maestro followed just behind me, but even with our twin candles it was almost impossible to see anything in the gloom. I recall something brushing past me in the dark and I stumbled away from the sensation in surprise. I knocked into Geppetto and dropped my candle. It rolled a few feet before coming to rest in some sort of puddle. I still remember how my heart raced as I stepped toward it, and I realized the puddle was a deep crimson against the dull packed earth of the floor. When I knelt to retrieve my light, a spotted the gray lump sprawled beside it.

My gasp brought my mentor to my side, and he added his flame to mine, revealing the carcass of the cat. The blood seeped from a wound in its belly. Whatever had killed it had also removed one of its feet. Upon closer inspection, we found the eyes were also missing. I hoped for the sake of the poor beast that the removal had come after death, but something about the way it had shrieked cast the shadow of doubt.

It was too dark to get a proper idea of what had occurred, so we resolved to take up the question again in the morning. My sleep was fitful and my eyelids heavy the next day when I buried the poor thing in the garden. There was no way to rid ourselves of the blood-soaked earth without digging up the floor. We instead settled for covering the spot with a rug. Geppetto called my attention to an open window, asserting that an owl or another cat must have come and gone. There were several strays in the neighborhood, and though even in the morning we found no footprints or other signs of a second animal, it seemed a likely enough explanation.

That is, until I set to work again on Pinocchio. On first glance I thought the reddish cast of his wooden body to be from the first application of the Maestro's powder. But as I worked, I realized some of pigment came away on my fingers in a way the compound never had. Oh how my fingers shook as I looked down at my hand and flecks of drying blood that clung to them. For several heartbeats I could do nothing but gaze in horror as the idea solidified in my mind.

When I finally tore my gaze away, it fell to the face of the marionette and its empty eyes. What was this terrible thing we had brought into being? I must have dropped Pinocchio then, for in a blink Geppetto was at my side and asking me about the clatter. He took the marionette into his arms and clasped it to him as if it were a crying babe, then scolded me for my carelessness.

I told the Maestro of my suspicions, doing my best to be gentle. For who would be more disturbed by this revelation than he? He gave a dismissive flap of his hand, but also moved a few paces away as if trying to shield Pinocchio from the pain of my accusation. I pressed on, showing him the blood on my hands and adding the weight of the unexplainable jolting within the mechanism to my argument, but he would not hear me. He insisted that we had failed, that the marionette was nothing more than a toy until we made our next attempt with the fresh batch of powder. Fueled by my pique, I tore the puppet from his arms and crossed to the hearth, shouting that if it was but a wood and clockwork rather than a living thing, it shouldn't protest what would happen next.

Geppetto followed, lunging wildly as I held the marionette above the fire. I held him away with my free hand as he cried out and clawed at me, but as the much younger of the two of us, I was able to keep him in his place. I lowered Pinocchio until the tongues of flame began to lick at the bottom of his feet. Even though I was making the assertion that the thing in my hand was in fact alive, I was not prepared for what came next.

A faint but distinct voice came from his throat, crying, "Father!"

Geppetto and I both stood there dumbfounded even as the puppet began wriggling in my grasp and kicking his wooden feet away from the flames. Neither of us could move until he spoke again. "Father, help me!"

The Maestro grabbed me by the elbow and yanked my body around. He pulled Pinocchio from my grasp and cooing his apologies, crossed to his chamber and slammed the door closed. Bewildered that my impossible hypothesis had been correct, I sank into the marionette's vacated seat and stared into the flames.

—

Geppetto had no choice but to accept that our creation was capable of terrible violence. However, he maintained that this was not through any fault of the marionette, but because of our lack of guidance. Like any boy, he said that Pinocchio needed a father to show him the way of the world. Children were inherently curious and mischievous, even those who were not born but made. I had to admit there was a logic to what the Maestro was saying. I had gotten up to a few things as a child that make me blush as an adult. We agreed at last that we should not continue with our mission to build any more living dolls until we determined if our first experiment could in fact be taught. And so it went that Geppetto turned all of his attention to the education of a puppet, and I took over the commissions to continue generating our meager income.

When I say all of his attention, this is no exaggeration. Over time, he became gaunt and pale. Pinocchio of course did not require food, and so engrossed was the old man that he would likewise forget to eat without my coaxing. Winter came and he shivered terribly, but when I offered to build up the fire and retrieve his coat, I found out that he had sold the patched-together thing in order to buy the marionette a book to learn his letters.

For all the tender care, the marionette proved to be a terrible student. He was not stupid, as I had suspected would be the case with a head made of pine. Though his grasp of spoken language remained somewhat limited (likely due to the mechanism provided), he proved to be both clever and lazy. He would often artfully divert Geppetto from whatever lesson he endeavored to teach, and the two would end up playing chess or some other game to wile away the hours.

I did my best to ignore them and concentrate on the business that moved in a steady stream through our door. Whenever a customer came to call, Geppetto and Pinocchio hid in his room to keep our secret, which only proved to make the wooden boy more curious about the outside world. Eventually, he got the idea that he needed a playmate, someone younger and more spirited than the elderly Maestro. The marionette harped on this concept incessantly, begging to be allowed to go out in the street to play with the other children (arguing quite cleverly that if he had to learn to act as a good boy does, he must be around good boys).

So it came that one day, the old man asked me if I thought we might want to take in a child. Geppetto cited his old age and the increasing numbness of his fingers as reason to bring in more help, but I knew that Pinocchio lay at the heart of his request. When I expressed my misgivings over how we would afford a ward, the Maestro used a combination of flattery and fact to convince me that I was such a talented clockmaker that we should never be in want, especially once I had passed my skills on to my new apprentice. I relented, and once assured he would find a suitable candidate who would keep the secret of the marionette, he set off to find a playmate for the marionette.

I do not recall the boy's given name, for he was such a skinny little thing that we immediately took to calling him "Wick." Geppetto found him in an orphanage and they were all too pleased to give him over to our care. We did not have another room for him, but Wick was content to sleep in the workshop curled near the hearth. Though our existence was modest, it was still a great improvement for the boy to have a home and a trade. He showed his gratitude daily with busy hands and dimpled smiles. I had not realized how lonely the workshop had become for me since the puppet took up the Maestro's days, and Wick's presence lifted the burden of my solitude.

Unlike Pinocchio, he was eager to learn and did not shy from any task we set to him, except perhaps his job as friend to the marionette. Though he was happy to keep our strange secret in exchange for the life we could provide, I could see in his eyes that he found the talking toy unsettling. They were by no means close as brothers as the Maestro would have liked, but they got on well enough for several months.

Then, it happened again.

—

Since my arrest, I have devoted much of my time to thinking about the nature of evil in both the general sense, as well as how it applies to my own sorry situation. I honestly cannot say if what Geppetto and I did by giving Pinocchio life was evil, though I know for a fact we harbored no evil intent when we did it. At the same time, one would be sorely pressed to find any good that came from our actions, especially anyone who saw Wick's body. I had the unfortunate honor of being the first, and it has haunted me in the days since. Perhaps it is a blessing then that I have so few of them left.

Unlike the incident with the cat, there had been no indication that anything was amiss. I had simply woken from a dream and wished to slake my thirst before going back to sleep. I tried to be quiet because I did not want to disturb the boy as he slept. The fire was low, just a soft orange glow in the darkness. Spring had arrived, but the nights were still cold, and I remember thinking that Wick would probably appreciate another log. I selected a suitable piece and gently lay it across the coals. The bark caught immediately, throwing a flickering golden of light onto the floor. Wick was lying on his back near the hearth. It took me a moment to recognize what perched on his chest, but when I realized it was Pinocchio I hissed at him to get away. As the marionette did as he was told, I saw the deep gash in the boy's abdomen and his glassy eyes, wide with terror.

The puppet looked up at me, and in his high, tinkling voice, he asked, "Where did he go?"

I dared to hope for a moment that this meant that I was mistaken, that Pinocchio was not responsible for the corpse at my feet. But then I saw how the blood covered his body, how it dripped from his tiny wooden fingers and the knife they held.

In that moment of horror, all I could manage was to ask him why.

Pinocchio looked down at the dead boy, replying flatly, "To show we are the same." The marionette tapped the trapdoor in his chest, leaving smears of scarlet across the polished wood. "So, I opened. But we are not the same, and I cannot close again."

Our conversation must have disturbed Geppetto, for his door opened then. He asked me what was going on, so I moved mutely aside to show him what our creation had done. The old man sank to his knees, and Pinocchio stepped to him and squeaked, "Papa, am I real?"

The Maestro gently took the knife from the marionette's hand, then tossed it into the fire. I found my voice, entreating him to do the same for the puppet, to end this mockery of life. We were fools to bring this homunculus into the world when we could not give it a soul.

He entreated me to let him leave, to take Pinocchio far away from people so he could continue educating it. I remember the tears running down his cheeks as he begged on behalf of the marionette, assuring me that with time and love it could be redeemed. I could not bear to have the thing near me a moment longer, nor to see my mentor suffer so, and against my better judgment, I let them go.

I will never know what brought the constabulary to the door that day. It could have been a coincidence, an officer who just happened by the shop and wanted to inquire about getting his watch fixed. Perhaps someone had heard the murdered boy's cries in the night even if I did not. Or, in my darkest moments, I believe Geppetto felt the need to silence me to protect his clockwork son. I doubt I will ever know, for my sentence will be carried out tomorrow. I harbor no malice for the hangman, for though I did not plunge the knife into the boy, I cannot deny that I am guilty.

At dawn I will dangle from the gallows, a puppet on a string.

Carlo Collodi, 1881

The Little Wind-up Mermaid

by K. Gray

Every year the mermaid had seen her sisters float to the surface to see what lay beyond the calm waters. Every year, one by one, her sisters came back to the kingdom with glowing faces, talking of the wonders they had seen at the surface. And then every year, one by one, they gathered together with the other sisters who had been above, chattering about the amazing things they had seen. This happened with all of her sisters, and every year she felt them drift further and further from her. The mermaid, the youngest of all of them, hadn't ever been allowed to go, and by the time her nearest sister had ventured to the surface, she felt entirely left out. They all had something to connect them, to form their little circle of tails and giggling, and she was left on her own.

She found solace in her collection. While she wasn't able to see above the water herself, things from up above constantly found their way down to her. Trinkets of every kind, from shards of solid, strong material her sisters called metal, to cylinders of wood, and shining, translucent stones. She collected them as she found them, drifting through the forbidden places of the depths, and returning to her secret, safe place in the palace. They brought her joy when her sisters ignored her. She could lie in her chamber for hours, drifting in the current and gazing on her novelties. She often made up stories of what they were used for, where exactly they came from. But everything in her collection was a question that was always left unanswered.

—

It was a year before she, too, got to see what lay above the waters of her home. Her father, the King of the seas, and her sisters were beyond excited for her. She was thrilled, too, but not because she would finally join the exclusive club that her sisters belonged to. The desire to join them passed long before then. Now, she wanted to see where all of her treasures came from. She desperately wanted to see how they fit into the world above.

When the day came, the entire kingdom showed up for the event. The mermaid was the youngest daughter of the King, and her coming of age was celebrated. She was decorated in corals and brilliant seaweed, given well wishes by the others, and danced around by her sisters. Her focus was still firmly on the knowledge of where her trinkets came from, however, and even her father commented on how solemn she was.

"You look unhappy, my darling," he said, and added a colorful starfish to her hair.

"I'm fine, Father," she replied, but her voice sounded far away.

"You'll finally be joining your sisters!"

"That's true," she said in the same distant voice.

He left her to what he presumed to be nerves, giving her a kiss on the hair. She wished she could be happier about this, but there was still so much she didn't know. She needed answers.

She joined her sisters and father shortly, but only after making a stop at her secret place and hiding on herself one of her favorite treasures, a small black oval with the profile of a person carved in white on it. She met everyone well, with smiles and greetings, and everyone that was old enough journeyed with her to just below the surface.

Her stomach roiled, like a school of anchovies swimming about, but she didn't let it bother her. Answers were far more important than her nerves. With a deep gulp and a flick of her long, turquoise tail she shot up through the warm waters of her home and broke the surface.

—

The first thing she noted was that it was very, very cold above the water. She shivered. The air here was thin, and it whipped around her, through her hair, and over her skin, sending little twitches and shivers through her. The second thing she noted was that she was able to breathe. It didn't feel like water, and of course it wasn't anything like it, but still she managed to take gulps of air. She wondered if that was part of the rite of passage, or if everyone had always been able breathe above and below the water. She took a deep breath through her open lips and let it out slowly. It wasn't natural, and it would take time to perfect it, but she could breathe. Another question, another answer she needed.

The sound of deep humming filled the air around her, and the mermaid swam in a circle to see where it came from. Looming behind her, coming closer, was a massive ship made of wood, metal, and that same clear stone. It moved slowly above the water, low enough to dangle some of its ropes among the rolling waves. It was massive – easily as tall as some of the reefs the mermaid routinely swam through. She stared up at it, open mouthed, until it floated so close that she had to paddle her tail and arms quickly just to get out of the way. As it passed, she heard thin, stringy noises emanating from it. She guessed it was music, although it didn't sound like any of the music in her world. It was still beautiful, in its own way, and it entranced her.

The mermaid followed the ship easily. It took its time sailing above the water, like a lazy whale resting after a big meal. She kept up, using one of the dangling ropes to keep her steady, and watched the tall ship for signs of these Humans whose treasures she had been collecting. Occasionally one would look out over the railing, and she would grin and wave, but they never saw her. She stayed with the ship for some time, listening to the chatter and music, and daydreamed of what it might be like to be up there, talking, laughing, and dancing.

—

As the sun set over the water, a wonderful sight in itself, the ship burst into all kinds of light and color. The mermaid watched the Humans light little boxes up and hang them all over the ship, including on the outside of it where she could see the flickering lights clearly. Their party (that's what she'd decided it was) was still going strong, and she was more than content to stay nearby and listen to all the new and exciting melodies exuding off the ship.

It was fully dark when the mermaid heard a loud splash in the water. She had been dozing against the rope she clung to, but the sounds of water and music from above jerked her awake. Thinking it may have been a shark, she dove headfirst under the water to escape. The smell of blood or shark wasn't there, but something in the darkness ahead of her made her pause. It was shaped like her, minus the bottom half, and sinking rapidly. She shot after it, her arms flat at her sides and her tail lashing in large up and down movements. She reached the creature quickly and grabbed its arm, but it failed to respond to her.

She had no idea if Humans could swim, but this one didn't seem to even be trying. It might be dying (after all, Humans never came down to see them), and without help it would at the very least sink to the bottom and face the dangers there. The mermaid drew up her strength. She took the Human under the arms and lashed her tail under the both of them. They rose to the surface in a matter of moments, breaking through the lulling waves. They both took large lungfuls of air, but the Human didn't open its eyes.

The ship hadn't seemed to notice one of its Humans was missing, and it had kept floating along without pausing. It was now far enough away, and the mermaid was so burdened by the Human she carried, that there was little chance of catching up and getting its attention.

The Human couldn't go back down with her. From the look of it, it wouldn't survive down there, so there was no taking it home to rest. Besides that, her father the King didn't particularly like outsiders. Even the old inventor wasn't allowed within the kingdom borders, and he had once been a subject of the King. No, she couldn't take him there. She didn't know these waters incredibly well, but if you went in any direction, eventually you would find large mounds of sand that rose high above the water. She would take him there.

The mermaid kept the Human's head above the water, and followed the course of the airship as best she could. It was a very long swim, but she wasn't going to let this Human drown. Especially not on her first time ever to the surface. And if it awoke soon, it might even be able to answer some of her questions. The ship stayed just barely in sight for a little while, but then eventually it sailed beyond the curve of the horizon and the mermaid was left in the dark, calm waters on her own with the Human.

While they traveled, she sang to it gently, telling it of places underneath the surface, and humming soft melodies. The Human stirred once or twice, but stayed quiet with its eyes closed. She kept singing to it, just softly, both to see if it would respond, and to keep herself entertained while she swam.

—

Land appeared just at sunrise. She saw the sun, the giant ball of glorious light, coming up over land. The sands rose high into hills and trenches, and as the light hit them the greenery dazzled to life. The mermaid, exhausted from her efforts, flicked her tail one more time and sped toward the shore.

Unable to carry the Human any further, the mermaid pushed it onto the land, away from the rolling waves. They didn't bother her, but made the Human sputter as they hit it, so she made sure to push it completely out of their way.

In the light, she took a better look at it. The Human might have been a him. It had similar features to the men in her world, but not completely the same, and when she peered under its drapings it lacked the breasts she had as a female. Not to mention there was certainly no tail to speak of, and that might have been the strangest part of all. But the mermaid resolved to think of it now as him, until told otherwise.

She brushed his hair from his face. He was quite handsome, even if he lacked the subtle scales and eyebrow ridges of the men in her life, and he was breathing. The mermaid leaned close to sing to him, to coax him back to life. She brushed his cheek with her hand, feeling the scratchy beard and strong jawline. He groaned softly and squeezed his eyes. The mermaid withdrew her hand quickly and leaned back from him.

As he came to, a thought struck her. There was a reason no Humans ever visited. Her father's words and warnings flooded back to her. She wasn't afraid of this Human, but it was hard to forget a lifetime's worth of warnings. Humans can be dangerous. Humans don't understand our kind. Humans frequently eat our kind. He stirred again, and the mermaid back away, using her tail and hands to walk herself back and away from him. Not far, for her curiosity was still at the forefront of her mind, but enough that she could dart back into the water if he grew aggressive.

He awoke a moment later, sucking in a deep breath and opening his eyes. The Human sat up, and nearly fell back over again, but caught himself on the way back to the sand. He pushed himself up with his hands, and brushed his long, dark hair out of his eyes. The mermaid backed away, slowly, hoping not to startle him further. Her heart raced. As he looked around him, his eyes settled on her, halfway in the waves, and he gasped. She flinched and scooted back just a little further, but her bright, big eyes stared at him in wonder.

The man opened his mouth to say something, but jerked forward and coughed. A shout came from far away in response, and the mermaid whipped her head to the side to see who else might be approaching. In the distance, down the beach, came more Humans. Running. The man noticed, too, and glanced over. He and the mermaid locked eyes for a brief second. Another shout drew his attention away for just a moment, and she was gone.

—

The mermaid darted back into the sea, using the waves as her cover. She swam frantically through the currents and the jostling waves back out into the deeper, open water, and didn't stop until the island was just a small lump of sand in the sunshine. She slowed and allowed herself to peek up above the surface, back at the island. She could see no Humans any longer, nor hear their shouts above the sounds of the water.

—

"Look! It's Lirit!"

The mermaid's sisters swam back and forth at the gate to the palace. They rushed her as soon as they saw their youngest sister, and danced about her in a flurry of hair and tails. She was exhausted, barely able to stay awake, but smiled as they hugged her hand gently helped her through the gates and into their home.

The mermaid's father was nowhere to be found. "He's out looking for you!" one sister cried.

"We've been so worried."

"What did you see?"

"Why were you gone so long?"

Lirit waved off their questions with a yawn. "I got lost… There was a shark."

That sent her sisters into a tizzy of gasps and chattering. It gave the mermaid a moment to escape, and she headed off toward her secret room. More than anything she wanted food and to sleep for the next dozen tides. Her room was calm and quiet, and the mermaid could think and relax. Her entire body ached from tip to tail, and she sank to the sea floor in her room. She fell asleep quickly, letting the sounds of water against her treasures from the Humans take her away.

She dreamt of the airship. Of the Humans and the one she rescued. Parties with strange music and flickering lights. All of her trinkets being put to use in their proper places, around her in a great open space made of wood and glass. She danced with them, on real legs, twirling around, and around, and around. The man whom she rescued caught her and laughed, and they danced together among all the other Humans, until the great sun rose over the hills made of green and sand.

She awoke some time later, in her little room, with an idea.

—

"My little song!" The mermaid's father bellowed as she emerged into the palace at large. He took her up in a hug and stroked her hair. "You were gone so long, little one."

She smiled and kissed his cheek, and gently extricated herself from his hug. "It was fascinating. And a little scary. I just needed to rest."

He nodded knowingly. "Ah, yes. The surface can be frightening. You don't need to see it often, if you don't want to."

Lirit smiled at him and nodded her head. "We'll see. After the events of yesterday, I think I'd like to spend some time on my own."

The mermaid often wandered on her own, and her father thought nothing of it. Just his daughter doing what she did best. He kissed her hair and wished her well, and she (along with a few bites of breakfast) wandered out of the palace walls. She let herself wander aimlessly for a while, lost in thought. The airship and her daring rescue still sat in the front of her mind, and no matter what else she drifted to, she always came back to her adventure the day before. Eventually her thoughts transformed into fantasy, and as she swam further and further from the palace, so did her thoughts go further and further into dreams.

Lirit gasped and came to a stop in the water. Her daydreaming had put her on the airship, with her Human. She could do it. She could meet him, and talk to him, and ask him all the questions she had always wanted answers to. But how to get there? She couldn't move well on land, even if she could breathe there. Of course! The Inventor! He always had crazy ideas, especially about the Humans. That was half the reason he was kicked out in the first place!

The mermaid flicked her tail and sped off. The Inventor's home wasn't that far out of the way. She could go see him, get some ideas, and make it home before her father or sisters had any idea about what she was doing.

—

When she arrived at the entrance to the cave, her stomach filled with eels. She paused just outside, swimming back and forth slowly, weighing her options. He wasn't the nicest of people, and according to her father he was actually crazy. But he had never been malicious. At least, she was fairly sure. There were a lot of details about his time in the kingdom that she had never been allowed to know.

"Come in, my dear," came a voice from deep inside the cave. It echoed off the walls and the mermaid gasped. "I see you there, swimming about. Don't hang about the door, it's rude."

Lirit swallowed. She hesitated, took a deep breath, and swam inside. It was dark, but she could see light up ahead, just little pricks of it, and they moved about swiftly. She put one hand on the wall of the cave and let it guide her in. Her nervousness grew every few feet, but the light grew stronger and brighter the further she went in, and she followed it.

She came into a large cavern, illuminated in pockets from above and to the sides. She saw now that the lights were little bioluminescent fish, swimming about in schools. They provided enough light to see by, and she smiled to herself. The cavern was quite large, and it was filled along every wall. There were pieces of humanity scattered all over the place, including large piles that ran up the cavern walls. They shone when the fish passed them by, and Lirit could see things she recognized, as well as a lot she didn't. It was like her collection, but a hundred times over, and her eyes were dazzled.

"Well now, there you are," the voice said again. It didn't echo as much anymore, and to the mermaid it sounded thin and rough.

The Inventor appeared, crawling from the back of the cavern. He had started as a merman, like her father and the other men in the kingdom, but that was just the underneath. Eight mechanical legs moved for him. They seemed to be attached at different points on his body, and he was held up in the middle of all the rusted parts by netting and metal sticks Lirit thought might have been called "tubes." He had fins like she did, but they were scarred, torn up, useless for swimming. His eyes were large and wide, and atop his bald head sat a pair of broken goggles. Lirit backed up a little as he approached, and he smiled with small, sharp teeth.

"Don't be afraid, my dear," he said gently. "I'm not going to hurt you. Although I'm sure you've heard many, many times that I might."

The mermaid shook her head, her long, red hair moving gently behind her. "Sorry, sir. I didn't mean to disturb you. I just—" She stopped. Was this really a good idea?

"You just... what?" he asked. Two of his metal tentacles idly picked up things from the floor as he moved and stuck to their pointed feet. He came close to the mermaid, and his real arm snaked up and took her chin in its grasp. "Sure you came here for a reason. Yes, pretty, indeed. Smart. Too curious. You're here to ask me something."

Lirit pulled away and frowned. "Yes. I mean. I am, but not if you're—" She squared her shoulders. "I've been to the surface."

That seemed to be all the information the Inventor needed. He smirked and shuffled away, carried by his arms along the floor in jerking motions. "Ah, yes. You have questions. You have always had questions, but now you have glimpsed the knowledge, and you want answers."

"Yes. I want answers. And I know someone I can get

61

them from."

He paused and tilted his head to look at her. "Then why come to me?"

"I need—" Okay. Now or never. "I need to get on land."

The Inventor stopped in his tracks. He peered at her and grinned wide. He let out a laugh that scattered the fish and, momentarily, the light. The mermaid shrank back toward the entrance. "Oh! Oho! You need to get on land! And those floppy little fins won't do it, will they? Can't move around except to flounder back and forth! Make a fool of yourself!" He crawled toward her and stopped just inches from her. His arms stretched out all around her. "Well well! You do need my help, don't you? How are you to get on land and get your answers without it?"

Lirit's hands shook, but she glared up at him. "Yes. I need your help. You're an inventor, aren't you? Invent me a way to walk on land."

The Inventor was on the other side of the cavern so fast it made the mermaid jump. His legs worked overtime, scuttling along the rocky ocean floor. He laughed, his voice high and reedy, and it scattered around the cavern and every available surface. "Well my dear! Haven't you come to the right spot?! Ah, but what do you have for me? Surely I'll help you, if you give me something in return. I don't work for free, you know! I don't. I need to survive, the same as anyone. What will you give me?"

She hadn't thought that far ahead. What did she have to give him? Surely anything she could acquire he could, too, except... She smiled at him. "I'll bring you back all the knowledge I gain!" The mermaid gestured around her. "You have all these things, don't you? From above? What if I could tell you what they were all for, what to do with them?"

His laughter subsided quickly. He looked at her with those giant eyes and his tentacles worried themselves together in a muffled, grating noise. "You will bring me back the knowledge I seek." It was not a question. "You must promise me. Don't lie now, I'll know!"

Lirit nodded. "I will gladly bring you back answers! I'm happy to share any knowledge I get with you."

The Inventor grew closer, cautiously, and extended one of his arms toward the mermaid. She took it in her hand and they shook. As he pulled away, she noticed a dark ring on her palm.

"Promise made, promise made," he muttered, and sank down to examine a pile more closely. "You're going to need legs, my dear. All of them have legs. Well, some of them don't, but you will." He started tossing items across the cavern as he looked them over. A few went into a pile at his side, the rest into the other large ones along the walls. "Going to take me a while. Going to take you longer. Sit down, girl, you won't be going anywhere for a while."

—

She had never felt pain so excruciating in her life. She screamed for it to stop, but every time the Inventor paused, he asked her if she really did want this knowledge, and she thought again of the Human, and the airship, and all the wondrous things land had waiting for her. She could do this. She had to. It was the only way she would ever satisfy her need to know. So the Inventor continued, and Lirit screamed until she went hoarse. Even then, she kept screaming long into the night, even when no more sound escaped her lips.

The Inventor's eight arms worked furiously and quickly, with all manner of tools Lirit had never seen before and never wanted to see again. He didn't let up until he was absolutely sure everything was done, and even then, he didn't stop fiddling with things well into the next day. By then the mermaid had given up screaming, and the pain had mostly subsided.

He backed away from her and flung his wrench behind him. "Aha! I've done it! I've really done it!"

The mermaid didn't move. She was so tired from all the pain and effort that she couldn't even feel her legs , much less use them. The Inventor waited a moment for her to catch her breath, but sighed impatiently. "Come on, girl, get up! I need to see my success!"

She didn't move. It took too much effort to move. And

suddenly she wondered if of that pain was really worth being on the surface? But how could she go back now? She glanced down at herself. The damage was done. If there was a way back, it was probably far too painful to stand. Just like it was too painful to stand right now. The Inventor tossed his arms into the air and scuttled over to her. He put half of his tentacles around her and hoisted her up, having no care for how much it might hurt her.

Lirit stood, but barely. Without the Inventor's help, she would have listed from side to side horribly. But he held her up until she got both feet under her, and when she wasn't going to float away, he let go. The mermaid, if she could be called that anymore, wavered, but stayed upright.

"Alright, girl, listen," the Inventor said. "We made a deal. I expect you to stick to it! And remember those legs won't power themselves. You've gotta keep them going. First one, then the other. You understand?" He made a motion of walking on two of his eight arms. "Like this."

The mermaid watched, the tried to take a step. How her fins were supposed to move independently she had no idea. She stumbled and caught herself in the water. She tried again. The water made it harder to move now. Instead of flicking her fin and moving forward, these legs made her stumble and fall. She was a hundred times slower than before! How was she supposed to move on land and keep up with the Humans like this?!

The Inventor, ever-impatient, ushered her along, forcing her to shuffle her metal feet forward in the sand of the cavern. Her legs gleamed off the little light fish, and she watched them move as the Inventor pushed her out toward the entrance. Her eyes went wide as she got to the mouth of the cavern, and the mermaid looked up (and up and up) toward the surface far above them.

"How am I supposed to get there?!" she asked, worried. "I can't even stay on the bottom correctly!"

The Inventor clicked his tongue impatiently. "Do I need to think of everything?! Come now, come now..." With two tentacles he gestured behind him. Sliding out from the shadows came two eels, if they could be called that, for they were entirely mechanical, but while her legs were all metal, these creatures were wooden with joints. Their eyes glowed faintly, mouths agape and lined with small, sharp teeth. "They'll get you there. After that, you're on your own. And don't forget our deal!"

The mermaid was suddenly swept up into a swirling mass of wood and gears. She felt herself lifting off from the bottom and rising up through the water swiftly, fast enough that it was hard to breathe. The trip took no time at all, the light from the surface growing brighter and brighter as the eels shot her upward. And then they stopped just as suddenly as they had started, just below the surface. Lirit had to catch her breath there. But she felt the eels pulling away from her, and with it her buoyancy. She scrambled her arms and legs to keep herself afloat, and she watched the Inventor's helpers slink back down to the depths.

Lirit pushed herself to the surface. She sucked in the cold, salty air, desperate for a breath. She never thought she could be so tired from swimming, but her metal legs weighed her down awfully, and were hard to use besides. She kicked with her new legs and didn't get very far. But no matter what direction she looked, she couldn't see land. She pushed forward, knowing that it couldn't be too far, just over the horizon.

Her legs made it nearly impossible to get anywhere. The mermaid kicked and kicked, but it was no use. She could barely tread water! How were Humans supposed to do this on land?!

The sound of a blaring horn shattered the relative silence of the water. Lirit gasped and looked up. Far above, growing closer, was an airship. It sank down through the clouds, a wooden whale in the sky looming closer to the water. Aha! Maybe it could help her! The mermaid waved her hands above her head frantically. She shouted out to the airship and— and what came out was not "help!" What came out was a wailing cry like nothing she had ever heard before.

She cried out again, "Help! Help!" and the same thing happened. Her voice was merely an otherworldly wail! She gasped and heard the horn again, then the sounds of Humans shouting to one another. With no time to think on it, Lirit continued to wave her arms in the air. They had seen her! A rope ladder flung over the side of the ship as it lowered further down toward the water. The mermaid kicked her legs and swam out of the way of it, just to the side and not far. As soon as the ladder was taut, a Human, a man, began climbing down it, another rope tied about his waist. The mermaid waved her arms again, but sank further under the water. There was no way she would be able to reach land without the help of this ship.

The man, and she knew it was a man by his clothing, just like the one she rescued, reached out an arm to her. She grasped his hand and he pulled her forward. Her weight with the legs was enough that he hard a difficult time of it, but soon she was on the lowest rung of the ladder, with the man's arm firmly around her.

They locked eyes, and Lirit knew who this was. The man holding her was the one she rescued! He recognized her as well, and his jaw dropped in surprise. Together they were pulled back up to the ship by the crew. The man only let go of her once she was fully on deck and lying back to catch her breath. They sat there a moment, quiet, with the ship's crew buzzing around them.

"A girl!"

"A girl with metal legs?"

"Look mechanical to me."

"What's she doing in the ocean like this?"

"Can someone please get her some clothing??"

The man pulled off his coat in a hurry, and draped it over the mermaid's shoulders. She blinked and touched the fabric, pulling it closer around her. Everyone on the ship wore the fabric, and it was quite cold above the water, so she thought she might follow suit and accept the coat given to her.

"Give her a moment, gentlemen, please," said the man. He stood up and gestured for everyone to back away. "Fetch some water. And food. Who knows how long she's been treading water."

A few of the crew scurried away, like crabs, Lirit thought. Or the Inventor. She swallowed and looked around the ship. It was all wood, except for a few small pieces of metal and that same clear substance. Glass? There were men everywhere – doing chores, milling about – all casting her strange glances and staring. She felt her cheeks get hot and looked away. A man returned quickly with a large flagon of water and a metal plate with some kind of food on it. The one who rescued her took both and sat in front of her on the deck.

"These are for you," he said. His voice was soft and smooth. "Are you alright? Can you tell me what happened, what your name is?"

Oh no. No, she couldn't. She couldn't speak to him with that weird, wailing voice. But she had to communicate somehow. Lirit's eyes went wide as an idea came to her. She pointed to her throat and then her mouth. There were merfolk below that couldn't speak, and they got on just fine. Maybe it worked the same up above. She opened her mouth and pretended to talk, but didn't allow any sound to come out.

"She's mute!" one of the crew exclaimed.

The man waved him away. "Looks like it. That's all right, Miss. You drink this up, and I'll get you to a cabin and get some clothes on you. Whatever happened, you're safe here."

The mermaid nodded. She wouldn't say a word and was too tired to argue besides. She took a bite of the food offered her. It was... She wasn't sure how to describe it. Dry. Brown. But also fluffy and melted in her mouth. The water was strange, too. No salt to be found and a little bitter. But not bad. The man sat with her while she ate and drank everything, not realizing how hungry she was. It wasn't food she was used to, but it would do. And afterward she felt herself grow heavy, and her eyes begin to shut. After the past few days and all the pain, she found herself unable to remain awake.

—

When she opened her eyes again, she was in a very large room. Lirit gasped and scrambled back against the headboard of the bed. This was not her room! This was not her home! Her memories broke through her sleepy brain slowly, and the pieces came together. She was above the water. On land? And in a room that looked nothing like hers. Lirit felt around her. The wide expanse of softness, the fabric covering her, she had seen these before in art from above. A bed! An actual Human bed! It was quite large and incredibly comfortable on her new legs. Was this how they always slept? How delightful!

A knock on the door jostled her out of her discovery. The mermaid pulled all the blankets up to her. She couldn't tell the Human to come in, she didn't have a voice! But that didn't seem to matter. The man who rescued her popped his head in and smiled.

"Forgive me," he said. "Normally it would be a lady's maid, but I wanted to make sure you were doing well. Are you?"

Lirit swallowed and nodded.

"Excellent. I'd love if you joined me for breakfast. We can learn more about each other then. There's clothing waiting for you in the wardrobe," he added. "I hope it suits you."

He disappeared, and the mermaid looked around the room. Her eyes settled on the large wooden box and assumed they kept clothing in there. She swung her legs off the edge of the bed and stood up. And then wobbled and plopped back down. She hadn't had to walk on land before! Where was the water to hold her up? Lirit frowned and stood up again. She wobbled, but stretched her arms out to either side to balance herself. Alright, good. Then one step forward...

Her leg made an odd, grinding noise. She stopped, eyes wide, and looked down. They looked different, somehow. She hadn't studied them before, but she thought there might have been a few extra pieces now. And something stuck out of each of them at the knee. Had the Humans done something to them?

She took another step, and her leg made the same grinding sound, but not quite as loud. But she didn't falter much on this one. Lirit leaned her body forward and took another step toward the wardrobe. And another. And another. This wasn't so bad! As long as she kept her arms out, she hardly wobbled at all!

Dressing was another story. But she managed to figure out where her head went – and her arms. The whole piece of fabric covered her from neck to feet, hiding her metal legs. It was beautiful indeed, blue like the sea, if heavy and cumbersome.

Lirit had to carry the bottom of it in her hands to walk, and when she did, she listed from side to side until she found her balance. How silly of them to bother with so much fabric!

—

Finding the man proved to be much easier. There were so many Humans there to help her! One of the – she thought they might be maids – helped her to the dining area. Along the way she caught glimpses of the sea out the large, open veranda. How beautiful it looked from so high! And large. Good thing she had been rescued. That was much too far to swim without fins.

The man greeted her at the door to the room and helped her to a seat. Everything here was shining and off-white. There was a very long table in the center of the room with chairs (like hers in her chamber) all around it. Food lay across the table in piles and on platters – and none of it she recognized. She sat in her seat well with these legs and gazed around at all the art, the various lamps, and finally the man.

He took his seat, nearer to her rather than all the way on the other side of the table, and gestured to the food. "Please, you must be starving."

Lirit smiled and started taking a bit of everything, eager to try it all. Human food was so different! At least a few of their utensils were similar, and she had taught herself to eat with a fork ages ago. While she picked, the man kept talking.

"My name is Marius. You're welcome here. I'm glad we found you when we did. Oh! I hope you don't mind that I had one of my mechanics work on your legs. They seem to be functioning much better now."

The mermaid glanced down at her legs and then at Marius. She smiled and nodded.

"I'm curious to know what happened to you," he continued, "but you don't need to tell me. At least not yet." She offered him what she hoped was an apologetic smile. He smiled back, and it melted her heart. That felt very strange indeed. "I understand. Take your time. I'll have my doctor look you over once more this morning, and then please feel free to rest here as long as you like."

That was very nice of him. She wished she could say so, but she couldn't make those awful sounds again. He'd throw her back in the sea! She nodded and ate and delighted in just about everything. She could do without the dark brown, bitter liquid, but almost everything else was delicious. Marius talked to her the whole meal, apparently wanting to keep her entertained. He asked her questions and she nodded yes and no, but when he asked her name she frowned.

"You don't know?" She made a face and nodded. "You do know, but obviously you can't tell me. Right." He tapped his chin. "I suppose I could guess!"

While he thought of a few names, Lirit ate a little more. He would never guess her name, she knew. But it would be fun to have him try.

"Is your name... Rebecca?" She shook her head. "Amie?" She shook her head again. "Irving?" She made a face. "No, of course not. Well, you were found at sea, maybe you're from one of the islands. How about.. Mariel?" The mermaid shook her head and sighed. So did Marius. "Maybe if you show me?"

Show him? Oh, perhaps like acting it out. Lirit nodded. That was a grand idea! But how to explain it...? She lifted one hand to her throat and made the gesture of what she hoped looked like a song emerging from her mouth. Marius furrowed his eyebrows. "Ah. Um... music?" She shrugged. Close. She did the gesture again and added little flourishes with her fingers. "Song? No, that can't be. But something close, yes?" Lirit nodded. "Singer, no. Song, no. Lyric?" Her eyebrows went up. "No, no... Ah, Melody?"

Lirit stared at him a moment, then shrugged a shoulder and nodded. Not quite right, but they could be there all day guessing. It would do. Marius grinned at her, and she couldn't help but return it. Smiling suited his face well. He clapped his hands and sat back. "Melody! What a beautiful name." But then he thought about it for a moment and pursed his lips. "Although if you can't speak..."

She smiled at him a little ruefully. She could sing! And well. Just not... above the water. Oh well. As long as he had something close to her name to call her by. And he looked so happy that he had figured it out. He beamed at her with a smile that would melt even her father's heart, and she blushed.

"Alright, now that that's out of the way," he said. "After breakfast, would you accompany me on a little tour of the place? We can figure out where you came from, and hopefully how to get you back home."

That was the opposite of what she wanted, but at least the tour might get some of her questions answered. She realized now that asking any questions about life on land was going to be next to impossible. Without being able to talk, how was she supposed to learn?

—

They finished breakfast, Marius asking her yes and no questions the whole time, and Lirit-now-Melody answered as best as she could. Some of her answers were the truth, as much as she could tell it, and some were plain wrong. But at least she was getting somewhere. It didn't matter if Marius believed her to be from some other kingdom above water, as long as she got to stay and explore his world for a decent amount of time. However long that actually was, she didn't know, but at the moment she didn't think much on it. There was so much to distract her!

Marius took her on a long and winding tour of his palace. She assumed it was his palace since everyone who greeted him did so with a great amount of respect; as much as she would get in her own home. How lucky to have rescued and been rescued by a prince! But she also nodded politely and smiled at everyone. Her legs drew quite a lot of attention, but no one stared for too long. And the more she used them, the better she grew at walking. Soon she was keeping up with Marius with little problem. Just the odd stumble here and there.

He showed her the layout of the palace; the grand ballroom; the kitchens; all of the major living and entertaining areas; and, of course, all the views of the ocean. Lirit noted that they passed a set of double doors quite often in their back and forths, and eventually she brought her legs to a stop in front of them. She gazed up at them curiously. The prince paused beside her and frowned.

"Ah, forgive me," he said. "It's been ages since I've been in there. The library." She gave him a quizzical look and he laughed. "You're very expressive! No, it's not a horrible sob story. It just happened to be my mother's favorite room, and she passed on some time ago now."

Lirit frowned. Oh, that would explain it. Her father didn't enjoy going to the areas her mother liked best, either. She put her hand on his shoulder, nodded, and turned to head back down the corridor. But Marius didn't follow. Instead, he grabbed her hand and swung her back around.

"Eh, let's just take a look, shall we?"

He turned the knob and the door swung open on squeaking hinges. He stepped inside, his boots clacking on the stone floor, and circled around the various pieces of comfortable-looking furniture for the windows. He pulled heavy, dark curtains aside and let sunlight flood in.

Lirit gasped. Covering every wall, every corner, and just about every table were books! She had some just like these in her secret chambers! She had spent a good deal learning how to read what they said. It had taken her a very long time, but eventually she had been able to decipher the letters! Of course, those thin papers did not last very long under water. Her books dissolved after a short time. Much shorter a time than she had to really learn what they said. But here on land, they might last forever!

Lirit stepped inside, her legs grinding softly, and looked around. She had a huge smile on her face, and she stopped in the sunlight to spread her arms and look around.

Marius smiled. "Ah, I see that you're a fan."

She nodded enthusiastically. He chuckled and bowed at the waist. "Then, my dear Melody, read to your heart's content. While you're here, use the library as you will."

She reluctantly let him lead her back out and onto the rest

of the tour, but she spent a good deal of time daydreaming about what could be in those books. By the time the sun began to set, she and Marius were walking along a stone path near the beach. The sun cast brilliant oranges and pinks across the water, and Lirit watched the waves dance along the shore. How beautiful everything was from this angle. So calm, so peaceful. Nothing like below. She wondered if Humans had any idea of what happened along the ocean floor.

Blinking away her queries, the mermaid looked over to find Marius gazing at her. She flushed pink and smiled. He only noticed what he was doing after another moment and turned bright red. He coughed and looked away.

"Sorry! Sorry," he exclaimed. "Got carried away. It's about supper time. Shall we?"

Lirit nodded, and together they left the setting sun for the dining room.

—

That night, Lirit had vivid dreams of sunsets, crackling fires, and piles and piles of books. She awoke to sunlight streaming through her open windows and the sound of seagulls on the air. A knock at the door brought her to her senses, and she opened her mouth to answer, but quickly shut it again. As the door opened, she flung off the covers and swung her heavy legs over the side of the bed. The maid that entered said her good mornings and immediately began helping Lirit dress, much to the mermaid's wonderment. She hadn't needed any help yesterday morning! Why today? Not that she could complain too much. Getting dressed in Human clothing was more difficult than she had imagined it would be.

The maid helped her into a very soft, very bright blue dress with little ruffles at the neck and cuffs. She quite liked the way it went with her hair, which above water seemed to be lighter and fluffier than it ever was down below. The maid also helped with that, weaving her hair into a long, elegant braid down her back. The girl bent to wind up Lirit's mechanical legs with the little keys that stood out from the knees. The mermaid watched in wonder as she worked, as curious about her legs as the Humans must have been.

The maid let her know the weather, the general news of the morning, and that breakfast would be in a little under an hour. And then, as quickly as she arrived, she retreated out the door. Curious, but Lirit supposed she had no idea how Humans woke up in the morning. This must be fairly normal.

Ah, but she had time! At least, she assumed she did. The ticking time-keeper on the wall told her that she would have time to find the library again before eating. She took a moment to steady herself on her legs, then began the journey back through the palace. The library door stood halfway open, inviting her in. Lirit stepped inside. She made sure to open all of the curtains like Marius had the day before, and then she started picking up books.

The first had far too many words in it that she didn't know. The second was almost half pictures! That was much better, and she settled in one of the overstuffed, leather chairs to flip through it. This was a book about animals, and Lirit took her time on each page, looking at the pictures, sounding out the names in her head. She had never seen any of these before! One page held a giant, angry-looking creature called a Lie-on. On another was something with a very long neck and spots, which Lirit sounded out as Gur-affe. She wondered if she might be able to see any of these animals in person one day...

"Melody?" called a man's voice from the hallway. "Melody, you're not in the library, are you?"

She blinked and looked up. Marius poked his head through the door and grinned. "Ah, of course you are." He strode in, pulling his dark hair behind his shoulders. "I thought you might have gotten distracted when you didn't come to breakfast."

Lirit blushed. She looked around her and nodded. Yes, it must be much later than she knew.

The prince waved it off. "No matter. Are you enjoying yourself?" He sat down in one of the chairs across from her and picked up one of the tomes. "There's so much in here that I've forgotten about. What are you reading?" She held up the book and showed him. "Slightly outdated, but not bad. It can be fun seeing all the life in the world that we'll never get to really interact with."

The mermaid nodded. She looked out the window and furrowed her eyebrows. If only he knew that she really had gotten to experience life in a world she never would have known about otherwise. She faced him again and smiled wide. An experience indeed. Her sisters would never believe this. Sitting in a library, with books, talking with a Human! It all felt like a dream she never wished to wake up from.

Marius grinned back. "How about breakfast, hmm? And then perhaps we can explore a bit more. Afterwards, you can come back to the books, and I won't bug you until supper."

Lirit nodded. She set her book down, and Marius hopped out of his chair to help her up. He chatted all the way to the dining room and all through breakfast. Most of it was telling her more about his adventures and the palace, but she answered more of his questions, too, with nods and shakes of her head. He seemed to seek out knowledge as much as she did. His enthusiasm about her and where she came from made her smile. So far everyone on land had been so nice to her. It made her wonder why her world and this one were so separate. She had heard stories, of course, of all the bad things Humans did, but nothing like that had happened so far!

After breakfast, Marius took her on another tour. This one ended much earlier, but also on the beach, and the mermaid spent a long while looking out over the ocean.

"Your home is somewhere out there," Marius said, more a statement than a question.

She nodded absently.

"I'll help you find it, Melody," he said. "Get you back there."

Lirit blinked. She turned to him and shook her head. That wasn't where she wanted to be! She had only seen the palace and beach! What else was there on land to learn about?

"You don't want to go home?" he asked, now confused. Marius was quiet for a moment, thinking. "You didn't run away, did you?"

She started to shake her head, then paused. She hadn't run! Well, exactly. She also hadn't told anyone what she was doing. Her father had no idea where she was... The mermaid hadn't thought about that before. Of course, it was her intention not to tell anyone, but she had to wonder what her father and sisters were thinking right then.

Lirit pursed her lips. She would go home! After she learned everything there, she would take off those silly legs and swim back to her father. Just... not yet. She smiled at Marius and took his hand in hers. She squeezed his fingers gently before letting go. His confused frown turned into a grin.

"Dear, silent Melody, you know how to keep your secrets!"

———

They finished their walk at the library, and Lirit went back to reading until supper time. Supper was much like the night before, but with more guests and more people to ask her questions. She spent most of it listening to conversation, doing her best to remember names, places, and the other things they spoke of. Everything she heard was so new! Kingdoms, the names of various Humans, what they were doing in their day-to-day lives – she would never remember all of it, but she was going to try!

The next day was more of the same. Marius seemed to cling to her a little more. He took her out of the palace a different direction this time. She met horses! Not like her seahorses, but ones with four legs who were very, very tall. She saw the airship she had been on before and met more of its crew. What a mighty thing it was! And able to glide through the air so gracefully. She had never noticed how loud it was before, amongst the noise of the sea. The crew all welcomed her, asked how she was. She received a short tour, walking amongst the men who took care of the large, dirty engine room, the rigging for the sails, and even the Captain's Quarters. And then Marius whisked her off to another part of the grounds. She fell in love with the garden instantly and was very reluctant to leave once the sun set and they needed to return indoors.

Lirit was happy to let the mechanic work on her legs. Happy to eat whatever the chefs put in front of her. Happy to walk and talk with Marius and the other Humans in the palace. She hardly noticed the days going by.

Except that they did go by. One day had turned into three, three had turned into five, with Lirit all the while ignoring the setting and the rising of the great, big sun, too engrossed in her adventure to care whether a week had gone by. Marius kept her entertained, and she dodged his questions and asked more of her own, in her own way. But by the end of the week a storm was rolling in off the water, and the Prince was getting more worried about returning her to her home before they were out of luck for a little while.

"My dear, I have a feeling we should be getting you back home," he complained after dinner on the sixth evening. "A storm will be coming, and they can last for days."

Lirit smiled at him and sipped her tea. She shook her head.

Marius frowned. "Can you stand to be away from home for so long? Won't they be missing you?"

She shrugged, the smile still on her lips.

"Have you sent any word to them?" he asked. "Can I send a letter for you? Tell your family you're in good care and need a little more time to heal?"

She shook her head again. It wasn't as if they could express their worry to him, after all. Or contact the palace. They didn't even know where it was. And he certainly would never know where or how to send a letter to them.

Marius shook his head and smiled. "So many secrets, Miss Melody. When will you feel comfortable letting me in on just a few?"

Lirit reached over and pat his hand gently.

—

The storm rolled in as predicted. The next evening, thunder clapped overhead, unimpeded by anything but the palace on the hill. The clouds rolled in, thick, dark, and heavy with rain. The staff clambered to get everything secure. The airships needed tying down, the more particular parts of the gardens had to be covered. The shutters needed to be closed and locked, and all the animals shuffled into their barns and stables and closed in tight.

Except that Lirit had left one of her great shutters unlocked, and she slipped outside onto the balcony to watch the storm make landfall. It was magnificent – beautiful and frightening. The whipping wind, the sideways rain, thunder and sparks of lightning, all of it happening before her eyes. She had to stay next to one wall in order to stay upright. Her legs were heavy, enough to keep her from being blown over in the wind that pulled at her skirts and her hair.

She watched in wonder as wave after wave crashed upon the shore. They grew so high when the wind was like this, and it fascinated her. She had seen a few storms from below, but they rolled over her ocean doing no more than making her swim a little more difficult. This was truly impressive! The waves hit the shore like hammers, driving forward the sand, pulling it back into the water. Lirit couldn't take her eyes off them and stayed there for several minutes, getting drenched in the rain and tangled in the wind.

Out of the corner of her eye, something appeared in the waves. A figure, way down below, dragging along with them a host of driftwood, dangling around them in the waves. Lirit frowned. Someone thrown overboard? How could they have survived in such a storm? She watched for only a moment before starting back inside to alert someone— and stopped.

That was not driftwood attached the figure. She turned her head and looked again, pushing her blowing hair away from her face.

She should have returned home much, much sooner.

—

Lirit tripped on her way to get the Prince. She hit the ground with a loud thud, her legs hitting the tile floors hard enough to chip away tiny pieces. "Help!" She shouted into the hallway, forgetting her voice would be nothing but wails. "Help, please!"

The maids were there before Marius was. They helped Lirit to her feet quickly, fussing over her and asking again and again what was wrong. She frantically pointed toward her room and the open shutter, and practically growled in frustration that she couldn't just tell them what was wrong. She brushed the two women away and started for the stairs, but Marius was already bounding up to meet her.

"Melody! Melody, you're drenched! What is it?! Did something happen?"

There was no time to try to answer him. Lirit shoved herself forward, hopping down the stairs on her legs, cursing the Inventor for not being able to give her something lighter. Or at least a voice! But she needed to get downstairs, to warn those at the gate that there might be—

Someone shrieked, and the sound of wind and rain was suddenly very loud in the stairwell.

Marius beat her downstairs. When she reached the bottom landing, the great doors were flung open, letting in the howling storm. In the opening stood the Inventor, upright on all eight mechanical legs, his mangled fins dangling to the floor without touching it. Affixed to his throat and covering the lower half of his face was a rusted old contraption that had three large slits in the front of the metal piece and two long, yellowed tubes running to where his gills would be. His legs, Lirit saw, were much, much larger than the ones she had met him in. These allowed the Inventor to tower over the Humans, several feet higher than any of them. Under those great mechanical legs lay both of the guards who had been stationed outside, even in this storm. They didn't move.

Lirit gasped. She held onto the railing of the stairs to stay balanced and stared at the Inventor. She had forgotten her deal. He had not. Marius strode forward, unafraid, and the mermaid tried to grab his arm to stop him, but she couldn't both hold onto him and keep herself upright on the stairs in the wind and rain.

"Sir!" Marius shouted over the din. "You are intruding on my property, and I demand you—"

The Inventor picked up one great, metal leg and slammed it down onto the tile in front of the Prince. The tile cracked and shattered under the force of the pointed leg. "You," came an unnatural, mechanical voice from the contraption at the Inventor's throat, "will not get in the way, Human. I want only what I was promised."

Marius took several steps back. He drew his sword from his hip, but cast a brief glance back toward Lirit. She was ghostly white and shook her head slowly in warning. "Whatever you were promised, beast, you cannot burst into my home and make demands! Surrender, or be arrested and tried!"

That didn't stop him. The Inventor moved forward, his great legs propelling him forward slowly, like a crab on unsure ground. But he kept moving forward. The Prince had to scramble out of the way to keep from being stepped on and pierced, his shoes slipping on the slick tile.

Lirit stood where she was, hands gripping the railing tightly. Her eyes were wide, her hair whipped around her in the ferocious wind. Had she really been gone that long? Long enough that the inventor came looking for her in a rage?

The great mechanical monster kept moving forward, one pointed leg at a time, although it looked like he had some trouble staying upright. He turned his eyes, behind giant, magnifying goggles, on the mermaid and took another step forward. With the same grating, mechanical voice, he spoke loudly. "We had a deal, yes, we did, yes. You promised to return to me, little princess. Lied to me. You lied to me." He coughed, and the mechanism over his mouth screeched. "I've come for what's mine. You'll give me your knowledge. Yes…"

Lirit took a step back, up the stairs, but she was still not completely used to her legs, and her winding was not really made to go backward. She managed to get back up two stairs before she slipped and fell, landing hard on the stair, her legs splayed out in front of her. The Inventor chuckled, though it sounded much more like metal grating on metal. One great leg picked up and came down for her. The Inventor reached over himself with one arm, and hit a button.

A great net exploded from the lifted leg. Lirit yelped, her otherworldly voice lost in the commotion and the wind, and she shielded herself from the net, but it was no use. The net swallowed her like a whale, and suddenly she was hauled into the air, wrapped up head to foot in the thick netting. She struggled against it, but her legs were no help and she couldn't possibly break it with her hands. She was swept up by the Inventor, whose rasping chuckle still echoed over the wind and rain. Lirit heard Marius shout to her, but the net swung too much for her to find him. She stuck one arm out and reached blindly for him, but she was so high up now, and too far away from the Prince.

The Inventor turned back toward the doorway, the net swinging from his lifted leg. He was even more unstable now, but his remaining legs clicked clicked clicked back out the doorway. By then, more guards had shown up, guns drawn. The Inventor scoffed at them. The commander shouted orders, and both Lirit and the Inventor watched the soldiers raise their firearms.

Right before the order to fire, the Inventor raised the net the mermaid was held in and rasped, "I don't think so. Don't think so. Would you hurt your guest? Was she not welcome here before?" He made a coughing sound, but it came out tinny. "Humans. Solving problems by shooting them. Tsk tsk tsk, Humans."

And he kept walking.

The guards were dumbfounded. They could do nothing without risking Lirit, and none were willing to do so. The mermaid pulled the heavy net taut so that she could see out. The guards kept their firearms aimed, but no one fired. Behind them, she heard Marius's voice faintly, but coming closer. By then they were on the stone pathway that led to the beach, and she knew exactly where they were going.

But how to stop him? Home was the last place she wanted to be, perhaps, minus wherever the Inventor was specifically

81

taking her. But they were heading toward the sea nonetheless, and panic grew in the pit of her stomach. How was she to get out of this? Where was he taking her, and what was he going to do with her? She needed a plan, but it seemed impossible to think of one. The net rocked back and forth, and through the small holes in it she saw the ocean, its waves towering above them and crashing to the sand, tormented and angry.

She thought of Marius, sweet, kind Marius, and the palace, and turned her head to look back at it. All the guards had their firearms aimed, but Marius held his fist up. They wouldn't fire. The palace looked magnificent from here, and Lirit thought of her library, and how she would never see it again. Her library, filled with books.

Books!

The Inventor wanted knowledge. She wasn't sure he would or could see reason, but if he wanted knowledge, she could provide it! Oh, but... her voice. It didn't sound the way it did under the water. Would he understand her? The water grew steadily closer. She had to try.

She knew that she must have sounded awful, but she shouted to the Inventor anyway. "I have what you wanted! I promise! I have been learning about the Human world! I'll share with you! Please just let me down!" She swayed in her net as the footsteps faltered in the sand. He heard her! "Please, Inventor! I'll gladly share what I have learned with you!"

A pause. She felt him stop walking. She could relate. Curiosity often got the better of her, too.

She tried again to get him to pay attention to her. "I have read many books! Did you know there are just as many animals on land as there are in our ocean? I have seen pictures of lions, of deer, and so much more! I would be happy to tell you about them, please!"

The great mechanical legs screeched in the rain, and Lirit felt them move again, but not toward the ocean. This time she was going down, back toward the sand. He was putting her down! Her legs couldn't feel anything, but she knew the sensation of the sand below her, and the net sagged down on top of her. It was heavy, and the mermaid had to hold it up with her hands to keep it from covering her completely. But she was on the ground! That was something. The legs creaked again, and through the tiny holes she saw the Inventor's giant shadow shift and move around her. She caught a glimpse of his mangled fins, still dangling from the center of his contraption, like they were when she first entered his cave.

The Inventor crouched on his crab's legs before her, blocking the wind from this direction, and even the rain. Lirit shivered in the cold. "Tell me, tell me," the Inventor rasped, the box over the lower portion of his face modulating the sound. "Tell me what you know. What of these animals? What of the Humans' culture? What can you tell me, little mermaid, about how they live?"

She could do that! She started immediately, shouting over the din of the storm. The mermaid told him of the animals she had read of, the horses in the stables. She told him about the airships, and the palace, and all the people that lived and worked there. She told him what the sky looked like at dusk and at dawn, and how everyone had welcomed her and been so nice.

"They're nothing like what we think they are! They have been so caring. Even their plants are well looked after! It's been truly an honor to stay here." Lirit frowned to herself. "I never wish to leave."

The wind seemed to grow less angry as she spoke. The rain came down still, but not quite as hard. The thunder felt further away. Lirit held up the net, soaked to the bone, her legs stiff and unmoving, but she took a breath and continued. "Please, Inventor. I didn't mean to break my promise. I only wanted more time here! There is so much left to learn!"

The Inventor didn't say anything at first, and the longer the silence stretched on, the more worried Lirit became. She held the net higher and peered through the small holes, but all she could really see was a looming shadow and hear his labored, metallic breathing. She hoped her plan was working. If he took her back to the ocean, who knew what he might do with her. That cave held many more secrets than she really wanted to think about. But she waited, scared to say anything more that might make him continue toward the sea.

"Yes, yes," he seemed to mutter to himself, but it was the same tone and volume as when he had spoken before. "Nothing like we thought, yes... Not nearly as dangerous. Look at them, not willing to shoot. Not willing."

The shadow moved, and the mermaid flinched. But then she felt the net being lifted again, and she no longer had to hold it up to keep it from falling on her. Lirit expected to be hauled into the air again, and she clung to the sides of the net for stability, but that didn't happen. Instead, the net opened from the top, and suddenly the rain came in steady droves down onto her head. The net continued to fall away. Soon it lay all around her, leaving her in a pool of netting. She looked up, and the Inventor stood over her. From down on the ground, he was massive – all metal and gears, slick and shining with rainwater. She could see his torn and destroyed fins well from her vantage point. Whatever had happened to him must have nearly killed him.

One of the guards shouted, and as the wind continued to calm Lirit wrenched her eyes from the Inventor back toward the palace. Marius stood there, drenched, his guards still with firearms raised. She held up a hand to him to stay, then looked back at the Inventor. She found her voice again, and in what sounded to her like incoherent wailing, said, "Inventor! What else can I tell you??"

He looked down at her, and then his crab-like legs bent and he sank down toward the sand. The mermaid could not get out of the way, her legs heavy and unwound, but the Inventor did not crush her. He moved off to the side and crouched. His bulging eyes behind the goggles stared at her. "I wish to gain this knowledge. I wish it."

She blinked the rain out of her eyes. "I can help you," she wailed. "There are so many books I can show you!"

He seemed to consider this, taking a moment to look at the raging sea, and then back at the Prince and the palace. "I'll stay here. For now. Long enough to learn. I'm going to stay."

That... was unexpected. Lirit looked up at the Inventor

with wide eyes. Her hair lay plastered to her head, but the rain was still lessening. "You.. want to stay in the palace? To learn?"

The Inventor nodded. This was a strange turn of events, indeed. But if he had helped her to get on land and learn, the least she could do was help him do the same thing. It wasn't as if the books here were only for her. Why should she be the only one to learn anything new? Lirit slowly smiled at him, and he blinked and moved back from her. She nodded to him and turned so she could see Marius and the guard. Lirit pointed to Marius and waved him over.

Slowly, very slowly and with sword drawn, he made his way through the wind and sand over to the pair. The mermaid smiled wider and beckoned him over faster. The Inventor backed away, his lower half dragging through the wet sand.

"Melody!" Marius said as he neared her. He eyed the giant mechanical Inventor warily and never dropped his sword. "Melody, are you alright? What's going on?!"

She gestured from herself to the Inventor. Curse her inability to speak to him. If she could just explain, just tell him—

The Inventor cleared his throat, and both the Prince and mermaid turned their heads. "If I may, this young mermaid owes me for giving her legs," he explained. "She wanted legs to get on land; I want knowledge. Yes, I want knowledge. She tells me there are books I can learn from. She tells me. She tells me she has learned much, much, and that you Humans are not so..." He paused, the speaker on his voice box crackling. "Bad."

Marius and Lirit glanced back at each other. She nodded emphatically. He looked skeptical.

"Melody," the Prince said slowly. "Is he saying that you are a... a mermaid?"

She nodded again, this time looking a little sheepish.

"Need to do something about that voice," the Inventor said in the tone that meant he was talking to himself.

Lirit blushed and reached out for Marius's hand. The Prince took it, looking very confused, but unafraid. She squeezed it, and pointed from the Inventor to the palace.

"Yes, yes. I want in there. I want to learn," said the

Inventor.

Marius stood again, and motioned for his guards. "Take Miss Melody inside. See that she gets dry and wind her legs. And..." He looked toward the hulking form of the Inventor. "Provide a room for this... this... Man. There has been a big misunderstanding, and it's going to be remedied."

Lirit grinned wide. She held her arms up to Marius, and he embraced her, squeezing tightly before letting go to let the guards escort her back into the palace. As they approached the Inventor, he scurried back in the sand, arms up. But the mermaid held up her hands to him and smiled. He relaxed and allowed the guards to lead him back toward the palace.

The group marched together, and as they reached the stone path at the edge of the sand, the rain trickled to a stop. The clouds began to part, relieving them of the biting wind. Lirit leaned her head back and smiled. Marius took her hand and walked beside her as the guards carried her up the steps and into the palace.

Treasure

by Crysta K. Coburn

Once in a far off land, there was a King who dreamed of having a child with his beloved Queen. In his eyes, she was the most beautiful person in the world. Surely, any child of hers would also be the most beautiful, and he would love his Queen and their child, and they would be the happiest of families. But the years went by, and no child was born.

One day, while out riding, the King and Queen, who had not given up hope of being so blessed, were talking together of the child they would have.

"She will have the shining black hair of her mother!" declared the King.

"And the spark of the stars in her eyes, just like her father," answered the Queen.

"And soft, golden skin – a child blessed by the sun," added the King.

"She will be grace itself when she moves," said the Queen.

"And sing like a bird!" rejoined the King.

"Our treasure," sighed the Queen.

Soon the royal party came upon a traveling show that had pulled their caravan into a clearing at the side of the road. They stopped to watch the performance.

First, there was a man who danced with fire and breathed out jets of flame into the audience that had gathered. Then out came a woman who spun large silver hoops around her waist, wrists, and ankles, not once letting them fall. But the spectacle that made the King sit straighter in his saddle was an automaton, as they were told, who could dance and sing just like a real girl. She did not even need any winding.

The automaton girl was carried out on a cushion and set before the captivated audience. At first, she did nothing. Then her head lifted, the hood of her cloak fell back, her delicate mouth opened, and she began to sing with the sweetest, most gentle voice, just like a bird. With her head and face exposed, the King could see her raven-black hair, eyes that glittered like stars, and skin that shone supple and golden in the afternoon sun.

By the time the automaton girl had shifted gears and risen to her feet to dance, the King had turned to his Queen and exclaimed in a hushed voice (so as not to disturb the performance): "It's our child!"

The Queen looked at the dancing automaton with bewilderment... and foreboding.

When the show was finished, the King ordered the leader of the troupe to be brought before him, and he demanded that the automaton girl be turned over to his care.

The leader was stunned and protested, "Majesty, far be it from me, a humbling traveling performer, to deny you, my King, of anything. But this automaton is precious to us. People come from miles to see her. Why will they come if she goes away? How can you ask us to give up our livelihood?"

The King surveyed the performers, who had drawn near out of curiosity and concern.

"I am not unsympathetic," answered the King. "Your girl is also precious to me! She is the child my Queen and I have dreamed of! But I see you are unpersuaded. Perhaps this will help."

The King went to the Queen and removed her gold necklace that was inlaid with rubies, emeralds, and pearls.

"A treasure," said the King, "for a treasure."

The Queen was shocked that the King would go so far for such as fancy, but said nothing as she was not accustomed to contradicting him in front of their subjects.

With obvious reluctance, the leader of the troupe accepted the priceless necklace, and the automaton girl was lifted onto the King's horse where he cradled her before him.

At the palace, the automaton girl was given her own rooms and servants. The King lavished her with fine gowns, combs, and jewels fit for a princess. He gave her the name Treasure for, as he often said, she was his dearest treasure.

Treasure was an obedient daughter to the King and Queen, always saying, "Yes, Father" and "Yes, Mother," never causing them the slightest trouble, always doing as asked. She sang and danced for her adopted parents and their guests at feasts and parties, charming all who met her. All but the Queen, who grew jealous of the attention the girl received, a girl who was not even their own flesh and blood.

In the way of the world, the peaceful days of the kingdom did not last, and one day, the King had to leave to lead his troops into battle. While he was away, the Queen conspired against Princess Treasure. All the Queen heard at court was how well-behaved the Princess was, how graceful, how talented, how beautiful. More so than herself?

One day, fed up, the Queen turned to a serving boy and demanded:

> *"You there, serving in my hall,*
> *Who is the most beautiful lady of all?"*

Frightened, the boy replied, "Your majesty is most beautiful!"

The Queen grinned, but then the boy added, "However, the young Princess with her dark hair, golden skin, and starry eyes is the most wondrous I have ever seen."

Enraged, the Queen chased him until he escaped her by diving into the kitchen.

It was outside the kitchen that the Queen spied a scullery maid. She pounced on the girl, crying:

"You there, serving in my hall,
Who is the most beautiful lady of all?"

Terrified, the girl replied, "Your majesty, of course, is most beautiful!"

"Finally," the Queen sighed.

Her relief was short-lived because the girl added dreamily, "But I've heard that the Princess with her raven hair, sun-kissed skin, and eyes that shine like the stars in the sky might surpass even her mother."

"I am not her mother!" bellowed the Queen, and she chased the maid out into the garden where she lost her among the hedges.

It was there that the Queen encountered one of the gardeners.

"You there, serving aside my hall,
Who is the most beautiful lady of all?"

The gardener, surprised by her sudden appearance, replied, "Why, your majesty, surely you are the most beautiful!"

"And...?" the Queen asked.

"And, your majesty?"

"And what about the Princess?"

"Oh, the Princess is a shining treasure! Her ebony hair, shining skin, and jewel-like eyes! Her voice is like listening to Heaven itself! And the lightness of her feet–"

"Enough!" screamed the Queen.

The gardener ran off, and the Queen stormed back into the palace determined to get rid of Princess Treasure, who was no princess, but a devil sent to torment her.

After three days, the Queen put her plan into action. She

summoned the Princess and said to her, "My dear Treasure, it is such a beautiful day! Let us go for a ride through the forest."

"Yes, Mother," Treasure agreed, and a carriage was ordered.

It was a peaceful ride with no talking, for the Queen had nothing to say to this usurper, and Treasure had never spent such an intimate moment with the Queen, and therefore she had no idea what to do but sit obediently in silence.

After a while, the carriage came to the very spot where, it seemed so long ago, the King and Queen had encountered the traveling performers and Treasure.

"Look!" exclaimed the Queen. "Do you remember this spot? Stop the carriage! Come, my dear, let us go for a walk."

The clearing was rather less clear, filled to waist-height with wildflowers and butterflies.

"Let us pick flowers," proposed the Queen. When Treasure began to gather the flowers, the Queen said, "Oh, no, not the sad and dusty ones by the road. Let us go toward the forest."

"Yes, Mother," she answered.

And so, Treasure followed the Queen obediently further and further way from the carriage, and then, urged on by "It's so lovely, let us go just a bit further," deeper into the forest.

When they came to a river, the Queen said to Treasure, "Wait here for me a moment. I saw some lilies over there that I want to pick. I'll return shortly – don't wander off!"

"Yes, Mother."

The Queen disappeared, and Treasure waited obediently for her return. But the Queen did not return. Unknown to Treasure, the Queen returned to the carriage and pretended to be distraught, telling the coachmen that Princess Treasure had wandered off and could not be found. When the men went to search, the Queen sent them in the opposite direction of where Treasure waited patiently by the river.

Night fell and still Treasure waited, but she grew worried. Had the Queen become lost? Treasure decided to retrace their steps and return to the road where they had left the carriage. But it was dark and she couldn't see well. She did not find the road and wandered the forest all night. She stumbled in the darkness and injured her ankle, causing her to limp.

The next morning, she came upon a small cottage. She knocked at the door and peered in the windows, but no one was home. The door was not bolted, so she entered the little one-room home. She saw there were dishes in the sink, clumps of dirt on the floor, and the bed was untidy. Remembering her days traveling with the performing troupe, Treasure set about cleaning and sweeping the home.

It was difficult getting around with the injured ankle, so when her work was done, Treasure sat in a chair at the table and rested.

In the early evening, a tinkerer came whistling through the forest, returning from selling her wares in a nearby town. The cottage was hers, and she was quite astounded to find Treasure sitting at her table.

Minding her manners, the Princess rose and curtsied to the tinkerer, who immediately noticed the injured ankle.

"Sit, sit," the woman commanded. "Are you the one who has tidied my house?" When Treasure answered yes, she continued, "Then I must repay you by setting your ankle to right. And while I work, you must tell me your story."

The tinkerer pulled out her tools and sat on the floor at Treasure's feet fixing while the automaton Princess told her all about performing with the troupe, being taken by the King and turned into a princess, and how she'd waited for the Queen, but never saw her – or the carriage – again.

The tinkerer, who introduced herself as Ana, correctly surmised that the Queen had intended Treasure harm and left her on purpose.

"I see your eyes are wide with innocence," said Ana, "but I think it best if you stay here with me for now. Tomorrow, I will go back into town and see what information I can learn."

Treasure agreed to stay. She liked Ana, and with the King away, she feared she had no friends at the palace if what Ana suspected were indeed true.

Ana made up a bed for Treasure to rest in as, so the tinkerer said, "Even automatons must rest their gears."

"Yes, of course," Treasure agreed. At the palace, she had a soft bed that she sank into every night. The bed at the cottage served its purpose just as well.

The next day, Ana returned to town while Treasure remained at the cottage. Wanting to pass the time productively, Treasure did the washing and chopped wood for the fireplace and stove.

Midway through the day, an old woman passed by the cottage, heard the activity, and stopped to beg for a few coins or a meal. She was surprised to see that it was a golden-skinned girl with glittering eyes wielding the hatchet. Fearful, the old woman scampered away, stopping only when she left the forest and came upon the palace. After telling the guards what she had seen, the old woman was brought before the Queen, where she was asked to repeat her story.

The Queen, while seething inside that the Princess had been found whole and well, maintained a calm exterior.

"Oh!" the Queen exclaimed with all the emotion she could muster. "It sounds like our dear Treasure, who has gone missing. But we can't be sure..."

The Queen made the woman wait while she went to her private chambers and retrieved a chest with a knob on the top. When she returned, she held it out to the woman to have a look.

"This is how we will know," the Queen told her. "This belongs to the Princess. You will bring this to the girl you saw in the forest and give this to her. If she can open it, then she is our Treasure. But if not, then she will fall down dead."

The Queen handed the chest to the woman this this warning: "Whatever you do, do not touch this knob on the top of the box, or you risk dying, too."

The woman accepted the box with great reverence. She was allowed to stay the night at the palace and treated to a feast such as she had never had.

The next morning, the woman again appeared at the tinkerer's cottage. Ana had gone away, and Treasure was alone.

This time, the woman approached and knocked at the door.

Having no reason to feel suspicious, Treasure opened the door and peered at the woman curiously.

"My dear," the woman ventured, her voice quavering. "My dear, do you have any coins or food to share with a poor old woman? In return, I will let you see what is inside this chest."

Treasure invited the woman inside and brought bread and cheese to the table for her. When the woman had eaten her fill, she presented Treasure with the chest.

Curious, Treasure placed one hand on the chest and the other on the knob on top of the chest to pull off the lid. There was a spark, a loud zap, and Treasure fell over the table, completely limp.

Well and truly frightened, the woman leapt to her feet, knocking over her chair, and ran from the cottage. As previously agreed, she returned to the palace and reported to the Queen that the golden girl had fallen over dead.

The Queen tutted. "She was not our dear Princess after all. I fear Princess Treasure may be lost forever!"

Feigning distress, the Queen retired to her chambers where, when she was all alone, she danced happily.

That evening, Ana returned to her cottage to find an inert Treasure. She rushed to her new friend's side, did a quick examination, then pulled out her tools. By morning, she had Treasure up and about, no worse for wear.

Treasure relayed the story of the woman and the chest, the latter of which was still on the table. Ana examined it and realized what it was, a weapon effective against humans and automatons. She believed it could only have been a targeted attack.

"From now on," Ana told Treasure, "I want you to stay inside while I'm away, and open the door to no one."

"Yes, of course," Treasure promised.

Some days passed and a priest was passing through the forest. He heard a most beautiful, heavenly song and followed the sound until he came to the cottage. He knocked at the door, and when no one answered, he peered in the small window. The holy man was shocked at the sight he beheld. A golden girl with eyes that glittered and gleamed sat sewing in a chair by the fire, singing while she worked. This was no angel, he surmised, but a demon!

He ran all the way to the palace and demanded a private audience with the Queen. He warned the guards to whom he first spoke that it was a matter of great security and urgency.

The Queen, who rarely was allowed to make decisions in such matters while the King was in charge, decided to humor the priest and invited him to meet with her over tea. What he had to say greatly frightened her. How had the chest not worked? How was Treasure still alive?

Rather than send the priest, the Queen decided to go herself to this cottage disguised as a beggar.

When knocking at the door resulted in no answer, she went to the window and knocked there. After a moment, the former Princess' hateful face appeared. She did not recognize the Queen in disguise and readily opened the window when the visitor mimed for her to do so.

"My dear," said the Queen. "Can you spare any food for a poor woman? A piece of fruit? Crust of bread? I have no money, but I can give you a trinket in trade."

Treasure went away from the window for a moment, then returned with an apple and the heel of the bread. The Queen accepted both and ate with pretend gusto, thanking the girl profusely. When she was finished, she pulled out from her coat a long, thin pin with a tiny diamond, one fit for royalty, set in the end by which the pin was held between thumb and forefinger.

"This is a hair pin," she told Treasure. "Turn around and I will put it in your hair."

Treasure eyed the pin, could discern nothing out of the ordinary, and obediently turned around.

With a wicked grin, the Queen lifted the girl's hair as if to arrange it with one hand, and with the other, she rammed the pin into the base of Treasure's skull. The pin was thin but strong, and the gears within Treasure through which it was stuck came to a halt. Because the diamond at the end was so small and all that protruded, it was hardly noticeable, even if one did know where to look.

To the Queen's unspeakable delight, Treasure fell down onto the floor and did not move, though the Queen called to her three times to see if she would answer. Satisfied, the Queen returned to her palace. Treasure lay quietly and unmoving.

When Ana returned, she was alarmed to find the window open, then to see her friend immobile once again on the floor. She examined Treasure and repeated her ministrations from the time before, but to no avail. Treasure did not stir.

Certain that this was the Queen's doing, Ana fashioned a sturdy box, placed her friend's body inside, secured the box to a wagon, and hitched the wagon to her mule. It took some days, but Ana and her package arrived at the palace, where she found a celebration. The beloved King had returned.

Though while the palace people celebrated, Ana learned from a serving girl at the river with laundry that the King was in mourning for the Princess who had disappeared in his absence. Ana took her mule and box to the nearest guard and demanded to see the King. When she showed the guard the contents of her box, she was led inside to a private courtyard. The King quickly came to meet her.

He gave a great cry when he saw Treasure's inert body and cradled her in his arms.

"You are a tinkerer, are you not?" he asked Ana. "Can you not do something?"

Ana shook her head sadly, then told the King what Treasure had told her of the Queen's actions and her own suspicions. Of course, the King was shocked at these serious accusations, and he immediately called for the Queen to be brought before him.

After Ana repeated her story, the King turned to the Queen and gravely demanded, "Is what this woman says true? Did you deliberately conspire against and kill our daughter?"

The Queen trembled. Lying to the King was a grievous offense. She decided to throw herself on his mercy.

"Forgive me!" she begged. "I knew not what I was doing.

You were away so long that I must have lost my wits. Now that you have returned, I feel myself again, and I would gladly welcome our dear Princess Treasure home once more."

"There is our dear Princess Treasure," answered the King, pointing to the box which lay open.

The Queen tried, but could not completely hide her triumphant twist of her lips at seeing the fate of her rival, and the King saw it before she could erase it.

"You have not changed," he said sadly. "You would attack her still if she were not beyond your touch."

The Queen bowed low before him and again asked for mercy.

The King sighed heavily. "You are my Queen, and love for you still abides in my heart, but you have betrayed me in the worst way. Therefore I banish you. Go now and pack. Tomorrow, you will be returned to your parents' house. I wish to never hear from you again."

The Queen hung her head. "I understand. You are merciful."

The King only waved his hands for the guards to take her away. He then sent for Treasure's former attendants to come and take the Princess away with orders to wash her, brush her hair, and change her into her finest clothes. He then gave orders for an exquisite coffin with a glass lid to be made so that he might always be able to look upon his daughter's beautiful face.

Ana was invited to stay at the palace until the coffin was completed and a memorial service could be had. She gladly accepted the kind offer.

The servants who tended to Treasure did so with great care. They knew her mechanical body better than anyone, and so, when one young woman ran a damp cloth along the Princess' neck and it caught a brief and tiny snag, she knew to investigate. She held up a light to get a better look, which made the tiny diamond sparkle. The serving woman retrieved a pair of tweezers and slowly, carefully pulled the pin, which was no longer straight, but twisted, from the Princess' neck.

The gears within Treasure sprung back into motion, and

the Princess blinked her eyes, confused as to how she had come to the palace. The servants all jumped back in alarm, then clasped their hands together in joy at the miracle that they beheld. The woman who had removed the pin ran to the King with the glorious news.

The King wept when he saw his beloved daughter once again up and moving. Astonished, but delighted, Ana gave Treasure a thorough examination, mending what needed restoration to ensure her friend was once again in tip-top shape.

"Treasure, my dear, Treasure," sighed the King as he embraced her. "Will you stay with me always?"

"Yes, Father," she promised. And, for the first time, she also made a request. "Might Ana also stay?"

"Yes," the King answered. "Of course."

And they lived happily all together for many years.

The Queen of Clocks

by Thomas Gregory

Deep in the Schwarzwald region of what is today Germany lay the village of Töttingen. Now, in those days, a town or village was known by what it produced. If you wanted chocolate, you went to Munich. If you needed arms, you went to Essen or Oberndorf. Töttingen was famous for its clocks and within the town was one master clock-smith to whom all others gave deference, and beneath him labored three apprentices, Siegfried, Klaus, and Hans. Siegfried crafted his clocks concerned only with their outer beauty, the delicacy of their woodwork and the brightness of their gilding. Often his clocks ran fast or slow or in awful syncopation. Klaus liked to claim that his were the quietest clocks in all of Töttingen, and, indeed, this might have been true, however they were likely the ugliest, as well, their casings full of pocks and scars, their gilding dull and tarnished.

The youngest of the three was the drudge, Hans, responsible for maintaining the clocks, cleaning the various parts before they were used, and setting the time of every piece within the clockwork's walls, all while tending to the same duties as an apprentice that were expected of the others. His clocks were neither plain nor ostentatious, neither too quiet nor too loud, and most importantly of all, they kept perfect time. Not only this, but so great was his regard for the old clockmaker that Hans found he could not let shame fall upon the name of the clockworks through the negligence of his fellow apprentices. Thus did Hans contrive to steal into the clockworks at night, the noise muffled by the snoring of the rotund Klaus, correcting the sloppy errors of Siegfried's clocks which caused them to fail to run true and buffing and polishing the casings of Klaus's clocks, sanding out their scratches and leaving their gildwork brightly shining. Of course, Hans tried to correct his fellow apprentices in their technique, but all that they saw were his constant yawns and the bags under his eyes, calling him "stupid Hans," and "lazy Hans," and "poor Hans who will never be more than a third rate clock-smith." Nevertheless, Hans persisted in correcting his fellows' flaws for the sake of his master.

It happened one day that the master clockmaker called his apprentices to the shop floor and addressed them thus: "I grow old now, and you have learned all that I can teach you. It is my wish to see the wide country with my own eyes before they fail me. Therefore, whosoever among you brings me the finest horse upon which to ride shall inherit the clockworks and all that goes with them." The clock maker then gave each of them a pot of money and bid them go.

By the time the three had reached the the outskirts of the farm country which bordered the town, dusk had fallen. The three were loathe to part with any of their money in exchange for a room in one of the farmhouses for the night and so counted themselves lucky when they came upon a ramshackle cottage which had clearly been the victim of years of neglect and whose windows did not show a single sign of life. It was resolved that they would spend the night in the forgotten cottage and to light out in the early morning. This being agreed, each made a bed of his cloak upon the floor and went to sleep.

Klaus woke just before dawn to a sharp poke in the ribs from Siegfried's boot.

"Wake up, fatso, we're going."

"Going?" Klaus yawned. "Going where?"

"To the city. Do you really want to take Hans with us to find a horse of his own?"

"Not really, no."

"Then get your things and let's go. With luck, the bandits of the forest will see him for easy prey, and our troubles will be over."

"But what if he should return to the village and tell the master clock-smith?"

"Who do you think he'll believe, two of us, his best apprentices, or one of lazy Hans?"

So the two set out in the early half light. When Hans awoke, he found himself alone, and as he stepped out of the old cottage, he found that not only was he alone, but also far further into the forest than he remembered.

It was then that Hans heard a strange music drifting through the trees. Time was kept by the ticking sound of a metronome, harmony by a thunderous brass horn, and rhythm by some many-stringed instrument. Seeing no better option for reorienting himself, Hans began to follow the sound of the music in hopes that whoever was making it might know their way back to the road. As he entered the clearing from which the music arose, Hans saw something wondrous. There, sitting on a log were three mechanical players. One was tall and shaped like a casket turned on its head. The casket man nodded his head back and forth making a sharp "tick tick" sound as he directed his fellows with a baton. The next was as big as a bull with brass horns sticking out all over. The tarnish on his horns reminded Hans of one of Klaus's clocks. Each of the horns gave a different "toot, toot, toot," or "tut, tut, tut," or "tump, tump, tump" depending on their size. The third of the mechanical players was thin and graceful, his body hollow in the middle, below the neck, and strung with strings of a hundred different metals and fibers and guts, half of which seemed to be broken. With one delicate hand he plucked and with the other he bowed at the strings.

All of them were driven by clockwork far cleverer than

anything Hans had ever seen, and there, in the middle of the clearing, most wondrous of all, was the perfect facsimile of a dancing girl, stepping and jumping to the music of the three players. Her skin, if skin it could be called, was all of hammered bronze except where it had cracked and fallen away around the right side of her face, leaving exposed an intricate web of cogs and gears and tiny flywheels. Siegfried would have been furious. Never had Hans seen anything so beautiful, so finely crafted, and so deft in its movements.

At his approach, the musicians stopped. So did the dancing girl.

"Ex... excuse me," stuttered Hans.

"Well it is quite about time, Hans," replied the girl, "it seems as if we've been waiting for ages."

"Ages," agreed the horn-playing machine.

"I'm sorry," replied Hans. "You see, it's just that I'm looking for the road, and my friends seem to have abandoned me in the cottage over there, and if you wouldn't mind telling me how you know my name?" The last part was not what Hans had meant to say but it spilled out nonetheless.

"Because I am the Queen of Clocks, and it is my prerogative to know many things, Hans-the-very-late-clockmaker, and it seems to me that if your friends were friends they wouldn't have abandoned you."

"Well, perhaps 'friends' was a strong word." The Queen of Clocks smiled. "Can you help me find my way home?"

"Yes," replied the Queen of Clocks, "but the road is long and full of dangers, and besides, it seems to me that there is little point in going there without what you came here for."

"I would settle for safe and warm even if it meant working for Siegfried or Klaus right about now."

"Do you dance, clockmaker?" asked the Queen. "I was practically made for dancing. In fact, I was. I can do the waltz, and the schottische, and the mazurka, and even the dance of Little Egypt. Would you like to see?"

"No," replied Hans, "I would just like to go home."

The Queen of Clocks sighed. "Very well. Come with me

and serve in my court for seven years, and in return for your service I will not only return you to your home, I will give you a horse ten times as grand as any your fellows will ever be able to find. Do we have an accord?"

Hans thought quite deeply about this, and while seven years was a good deal longer than he wished to spend away from the clockworks, he admitted that he was very curious about the mechanical people and their queen, and in the end, what choice did he have?

"We have an accord," agreed Hans.

"Then let us repair to the palace."

The horn-playing machine gave a sudden blast of all his horns at once, giving Hans a start. He heard the carriage long before he saw the thing coming through the woods, all steam and iron, pulled by a team of steel horses whose copper-clad hooves clopped and crashed across the forest floor. A wobbling, spring waisted coachman descended from atop the thing once it had come to a halt and opened the door. The Queen and Hans entered one after another followed by the casket man and the broken stringed thing, who squeezed in behind them. Hans found it somewhat difficult to appreciate the lush appointments pressed against the two players and their queen. The third player was far too large to fit into the carriage and instead scuttled along behind it, keeping pace on a dozen crab-like legs. As the carriage began to move, the Queen of Clocks reached across and drew shut the curtains shrouding them in near blackness.

"The way is long and full of dangers, remember?"

Hans nodded. Despite the fact that he'd only just awoken, he found himself drifting back to sleep.

When next he awoke, the midday sun was shining through the curtains heating up the coach. The conveyance stopped presently, and the coachman opened the door again. The castle had seen better days, but still held the ghost of its former grandeur. Huge spiral towers stood at three of the corners, the fourth of which met the road boasting a crenelated parapet with some form of cannon, once likely quite intimidating, now covered in moss and probably rather useless. The castle gardens, once presumably a verdant, manicured work of art now likewise was overgrown and threatening to overtake the structure proper, creepers trailing up the towers and blocking windows and wild privets and yews left to circle the castle base without regard for form or shape.

A small detachment of guards awaited them within the castle courtyard. Like the three players, each of them was in someway or other damaged, broken, or tarnished, and all, like their queen, were built of clockwork. As they fell in lockstep behind their queen, one of the guards missing an eye, an oily rag covering its place, stepped up behind her.

"Make a place for our clockmaker," ordered the Queen.

Rag-eye saluted and marched off to be replaced by another tin soldier.

"See that the cooks prepare feast."

The replacement guard saluted and it, too, was gone. One by one the tin men were sent to prepare the castle for a living, breathing human being, a sight that they were clearly unused to seeing.

The castle doors, thrice as high as Hans, opened with a grinding of gears and a squealing of metal as the Queen of Clocks approached. Inside, a host of servants was already busying themselves. Each of them bowed and greeted first the Queen and then Hans, some better able to speak than others. The floor of the castle was laced with a maze of thin rail tracks upon which they ran. Periodically, two or three servants would find themselves stuck on the same track going opposite directions and collide with a crash, or one would be forced to back up to the first switchback so that the other could pass, each apologizing profusely to the other. The chaos came to a clattering head as the Queen's head steward and his assistants all collided with an equally large group of perpetually giggling maids causing all of them to completely derail, most toppling over, and the steward jumping the track and careening into the wall where he spun in a tight circle. The Queen sighed as the retinue of guards returned from their duties to right the servants and place them back on their tracks. Hans and the Queen together guided the steward back to his place, as well.

"I leave you in the care of my chief steward, Hans. See that the clockmaker is taken to his rooms and prepared for feast." The steward gave a tight nod and began to slowly trundle along the tracks leading upstairs. "Try not to derail again before you get there," called the Queen behind them.

Hans followed the steward as he spiraled his way up floor by floor slowly enough for him to follow. His initial shock having worn off, Hans suddenly found himself full of questions and did not know where to start. Fortunately the steward started for him.

"My apologies, clockmaker, for the state of the Queen's palace. We are each bound by our particular purpose, and I fear none of us was built with the purpose of repairing the others, leading to the sad state of decline in which you see us. Ah, here we are." The steward rolled to a halt before one of the many rooms on the upper floor of the palace. Inside, two chambermaids waited, one on either side of the door. They gave matching curtsies as Hans entered, rolling off one after the other as the steward followed him inside. Hans wondered if he would, indeed, be able to find the room again unescorted.

The two maids had cleaned and dusted, made the bed, and set pitchers of water, one cold and one hot, in a matter of minutes. The windows had all been opened, and a light breeze blew in, billowing the curtains.

"Your tools, master clocksmith."

The steward showed Hans to a large workbench on the far side of the room. On the bench lay the finest set of clockmaker's tools that Hans had ever seen, all of copper and gold, and a magnifying lamp of silver.

At evening time, after Hans had settled himself in his rooms, washed and dried himself and dressed again, there was a gentle knock at the door. There, in the doorway stood the Queen of Clocks, dressed in full finery. Her skirts and gloves were a webwork of delicately woven chain studded with citrine. Her bodice was an enameled copper whose lace pattern matched a half mask that covered the damaged side of her face.

"Come, Hans, it is time for feast. I am sorry that we do not have more appropriate finery for you," she apologized as she led him back down the palace's winding stairs. "None, I fear, has been tasked to weave and sew. We do, however, have an excellent cook and many fine brewers, and bakers, and makers of cheese." And Hans found that this was indeed true as he sat down to a grand feast at which he, of course, was the only one who needed to eat, though the Queen, too, had a place setting of her own for the sake of politeness. After dinner had been cleared away, the three players, in whose company Hans had found the Queen before, returned and began to play. Despite their various mechanical infirmities, they were all three very capable and versed in many forms of music from various regions. As they struck up, the Queen left her seat and began to dance. After several reels and a brief jig, the players moved into a waltz, and the Queen returned to the table and Hans's side.

"Dance with me, clockmaker?" the Queen asked. Hans looked at the delicacy of her extended hand, the gears and cogs visible beneath her lacy half mask, and the elegance of her frame and was overcome.

"I cannot, your majesty, for you seem to me so fragile that I fear that you might break," he answered.

"Very well," replied the Queen of Clocks and beckoned her steward. "See that he is washed and taken to bed. Tomorrow he will be to work."

And so, Hans was taken to his room where he was bathed by three of the castle servants, one who washed over him water piping hot, and one who scrubbed him, and one who washed and dried his face with a gentle buffing wheel, which was very soft indeed. Then, he was shown to his bed, which had been warmed for him to a very fine temperature, and he slept more soundly than if he had been in his very own bed.

The next morning, his fast was broken with fresh fruits and pastries and rich, dark coffee, after which he was once again brought to the Queen.

"So, Hans, today begins your service to me. As you can see, there are many things which require a clocksmith's ministrations, starting with the royal gardener."

The Queen took him to the windows that overlooked the wild royal gardens. From above, they looked even worse off than Hans had initially thought, and there, in the center of the gardens, stood a giant beetle-like machine. At the end of each of its many arms was a gardener's tool of one sort or another, shovel, scythe, shear, and billhook, plus many that Hans did not even recognize. The garden paths were well overgrown, and even making it to the gardener would be a task. The steward outfitted him with his tools, as well as a small hatchet and, at the Queen's dismissal, took Hans down to the garden gate.

The steward threw a lever jutting from the garden wall, and the great iron gate struggled open with a grinding and gnashing of gears. Then, Hans was left to enter the garden, alone, his tools tucked into a roll of leather hitched over his shoulder with a buckled strap. The garden was lush, filled with heady floral scents from greenery allowed to run wild and decaying plant matter from seasons gone by carpeting the ground. More than once, Hans was forced to stop his progress and cut his way through briar, and creeper, and climber. By the time he reached the beetle-shelled gardener, he had lost all sense of time in the cloud of perfumed flowers and the sticky heat of the garden.

The gardener's shell was half lifted like that of a scarab about to take flight. Instead of wings, however, a myriad of arms, each ending in a gardener's tool like those Hans had seen from the palace window was tucked underneath. Two bulging round eyes sat above a mouth full of grinding chain teeth. All of it had long ago come to a complete and total stop. Hans unshouldered his tools, cleared a spot on the ground and began to work. He found the hatch that revealed the inner working of the gardener and cleared the vines that had grown inside. He crawled into the tiny space between the shell and the back and freed each of the thing's many arms. Those that needed tightening, he tightened. Those that needed loosening, he loosened. He carefully brushed the grit from the gardener's joints and oiled them again. Finally, as the sun began its slow movement across the western sky, he found the root cause of the gardener's distress, a central gear on the underside of the thing had come loose on its axle, causing it to wobble unevenly and preventing it from meshing properly with the other gears.

As Hans righted the final gear, the gardener came to life with a groan and a shudder. Its chain teeth gave a tentative grinding whir as its arms swung wildly. Shears clipped together again and again as Hans crawled out from the beetle machine's underbelly. Both of its bug eyes rolled in his direction and went wide. Steam bellowed from its nostrils as an arm swung at Hans, then another, and another. Sparks flew from the cobblestone path as another blade came for him. Hans threw his hands across his face, closing his eyes against what would surely be the killing blow.

The strike never came. Hans opened his eyes and saw the rag-eyed soldier gripping the beetle's sickle arm tightly in his fist as it struggled to get away.

"Flee, clockmaker!"

Hans ignored the soldier's order and scrambled up the beetle's back to where its head joined with the winged body. His fist hammered against the back of the gardener's head until a smaller plate came loose. The beetle-machine bucked as he gingerly reached inside. Very quickly he discovered the problem. Pulling his arm out from the gardener's head case, he removed with it a small chittering, windup mouse. Hans tossed the thing into the brush as the gardener stilled and it ran off.

"Oh, my. I beg your forgiveness, clockmaker," the gardener said, his surprisingly gentle voice coming from the hollows of his saw-toothed maw. "The mouse, you see."

The rag-eyed soldier released the gardener's arm and it retracted under his shell.

"My apologies, sirrah." Rag-eye huffed by way of response as the gardener suddenly noticed the state of his domain. "Oh, my. Oh, no, no, no, this will never do. The Queen must be so cross with me." All at once the gardener's arms became a whirlwind of motion, chopping, cutting, pulling, and digging. As it rolled off, apparently forgetting them, Hans and the rag-eyed soldier returned to the palace.

On their return, Hans repaired to his chamber, cleaned and replaced each of his tools as he had been taught by his master, and washed the grime from his face. Soon after, the Queen once again appeared at his door to call him for feast. Her gown was a web of fine silver, studded with sapphires. As before, a great feast was laid out at which Hans was the only one who ate. When he had eaten his fill and the feast had been cleared, the three players appeared again, and the Queen began to dance. Shortly, she approached Hans.

"Dance with me, clockmaker."

Hans looked at the Queen of Clocks in her silver and sapphire finery and thought of the dirty smock and rough trousers that he himself wore and turned red.

"No," replied Hans, "for I fear it would be quite unseemly, your majesty."

"Very well," sighed the Queen of Clocks and called for an attendant. "See the clockmaker to his rooms if you please."

Hans awoke the next day to a great thundering rumble. Outside his window, he could see a rain of stonework tumbling into the courtyard below. Hans dressed quickly and ran into the hallway to find the chief steward.

"What's happening?" shouted Hans, covering his ears to block out the noise.

"It's the castle masons," replied the steward. "The gardener dislodged them from the overgrowth and they seem to have run amok. They've put holes in most of the top floor already. Shall I set breakfast then?"

Outside in the courtyard, the Queen was already waiting.

"What are they doing?"

"They're trying to repair the tower," answered the Queen, "but their timing's all gone wrong. They should be moving as one, but instead they keep tossing the bricks forward without the next to catch them."

As Hans watched the builders hefting stones, slinging mortar, and raining bricks down upon the courtyard, he could not help but think of the big tower clock in the town square in Töttingen with its great Gog and Magog hammering upon the tower bell to mark the hour. Hans remembered going up into the tower with the master clocksmith early in his apprenticeship, as all apprentices did, to see the inner workings writ large and check their timing mechanisms, and this gave him an idea.

"Your majesty, I need the timekeeper from your players and your strongest guard."

"Of course."

A few moments later, Hans, the casket shaped player, and the rag-eyed soldier were high atop the castle roof. The casket man was noticeably uncomfortable, his odd shape making it difficult to keep his balance.

"Play," ordered Hans. The casket man began a steady beat, in time with the first of the masons. Hans and the rag-eyed soldier in turn took hold of the next of the builders in line, releasing it in time with the beat before grabbing the next and then the next. Soon, the masons were once again moving in harmony, and Hans was quite pleased with himself. For his part, the casket shaped player was simply glad to be back on solid ground. By the end of the day the damage done had been repaired, and the masons were well on their way to fixing the many long years of neglect that had already taken their toll.

So it was that each day, for seven years, Hans was given some subject of the Queen's clockwork kingdom to repair or set to rights and, each night when he returned, he was feasted and feted and when that was done, he was asked to dance and, just as on his first night of service, he found himself making an excuse as to why he could not. Then came the day when Hans returned to the palace only to find that no feast had been laid out for him, no courtiers had gathered in his honor, and no musicians were there to play. Now, by this time, Hans had lost all sense of how long he had been in the Queen's service, so accustomed to the routine of repairing the clockwork people had he become, so to find that his routine had been broken was very strange.

In his room, Hans found waiting a meal of sausage, and bread, and cheese, and barley wine, fit for a clockmaker's apprentice. When he had finished this, he went in search of the Queen. He found her in the garden looking very solemn.

110

"Do you know what today is, Hans?" Hans told her that he did not. "Today is the final day of your service. Tomorrow, my carriage will take you home."

Hans understood now her sadness, for there, in the kingdom of the Queen of Clocks, he had found purpose.

"But your majesty, I have not yet finished the work." Hans reached out and gently touched her damaged face. The Queen smiled.

"Dance with me."

And there, alone in the castle garden with no hint of music, Hans took the clockwork Queen's hand and began to dance.

"Your work here is done," said the Queen as the dance was finished. "Rest now, and in three days time you shall have your horse."

Hans retired to his room and soon fell fast asleep. He woke to the sound of singing birds and the smell of dust and mildew. He ached from the hard floor of the old cottage. Hans looked at his hands, once worn from his castle labors now as young and nimble as when he'd first left the clockworks. It was as if the last seven years had been stripped from his body. For a moment, Hans wondered if it had all been a dream, and, indeed, would have believed it so had it not been for his clothes. Though Hans had tried his best to mend and preserve them, he was by no means an able tailor, and seven years had taken their toll, leaving only enough for decency.

So, it was thusly dressed that Hans returned to the clockworks. As soon as he neared, Siegfried and Klaus appeared from within, having seen him approach from the window. On seeing his appearance, both began to laugh.

"You see, Klaus, I told you stupid Hans would never find a horse, and now he's managed to ruin his only suit of clothes as well, and in only a week. Some adventure you must have had, Hans!"

On hearing the commotion, the master clocksmith came from his workshop. And upon seeing Hans, he simply shook his head.

"What a shameful state you are in, Hans, and where is your horse?"

"My horse will be here in three days time," said Hans.

"Then you shall sleep in the stables until then, for you are far too pitiful looking to be seen in the clockworks."

Hans hung his head, but did as he was bid. To go from a palace to the stables was quite a fall. He spent the next two days grooming and feeding the horses with which Siegfried and Klaus had returned, one of which was toothless and the other half blind, though both were generally good natured otherwise, perhaps because Hans was in just as sorry a shape as they, and missing his warm bed in the Queen's palace. On the morning of the third day, Hans awoke to a great clamor in the street that ran in front of the master clock-maker's shop. A team of great snorting white horses clomped up to the building pulling a carriage even more finely gilt than one of Siegfried's clocks and driven by a coachman who seemed to wobble back and forth on his seat with every bump. From the carriage first emerged a veteran guard whose right eye was covered with a leather patch followed by two servants and, finally, by the most beautiful woman Hans had ever seen. The master clocksmith emerged from his workshop, followed by Siegfried and Klaus.

"Where is Hans?" demanded the woman. "Where is the clocksmith's drudge?"

"What would you want with stupid Hans," asked Siegfried, approaching. "Surely we can build you a clock much finer than anything he might cobble together."

"Shut up, you fool," hissed the master clocksmith, "can't you see you're in the presence of royalty? My lady, I fear that Hans is in no condition to appear before one such as yourself. In fact, so shameful is his appearance that he must sleep in the stables."

"Retrieve him for me," ordered the woman. The two servants did as they were bid, retrieving Hans from the stables upon which he immediately knelt. "Rise, Hans. You of all people have no need to kneel before me."

"Your majesty," replied Hans as he stood.

"I seem to remember owing you the debt of a horse, earned in honest and loyal service."

The coachman unhitched one of the fine white horses, leaving the team even in number. Siegfried and Klaus stood aghast, a lifetime of service to Hans flashing before their eyes.

"The clockworks go to Hans, then," said the clockmaker, "for never have I seen a horse so fine as this."

"No," replied the Queen, "your clockworks you shall keep, and your two dunces, as well. The hands that saved a kingdom have no need to toil further."

And so, the Queen had Hans bathed and dressed in fine garments, and in the master clocksmith's own chambers no less, before accompanying him into her carriage and returning to the kingdom of the formerly clockwork people, where together they danced and grew to be very, very old.

About the Authors

Crysta K. Coburn earned her degree in creative writing from Western Michigan University in 2005 and has been writing and editing professionally since. Her award-winning stories can be found in various magazines and anthologies, including *GlassFire Anthology*, *Valves and Vixens* volumes *I* and *II*, and *Cosmic Encounters*. For more information on Crysta and her award-winning writing, check out crystakcoburn.blogspot.com.

Phoebe Darqueling currently calls Germany home, but she grew up in Minnesota. When she isn't penning speculative fiction, acting as co-editor of SteampunkJournal.org, and sharing advice articles for her fellow writers on OurWriteSide.com, she is the Creative Director for a creativity competition for grades 5-8. You can find her Gothic short story, "The Vigil," in the *Chasing Magic* anthology, as well as her contributions to the novel *Esyld's Awakening*, which were both published by the Collaborative Writing Challenge in 2017. She coordinated and contributed to a Steampunk fantasy novel called *Army of Brass* that launched in 2018.

Bess Raechel Goden is the author, illustrator, model, designer and fiber artist behind SteampunkParliament.com, a steampunk themed shop and blog that has something for every nerd. She also writes for SteampunkJournal.org and runs the political blog DearOldPeople.com. She loves making handmade lace, drawing comics, coloring, and singing to herself. Subscribe to SteampunkParliament.com for freebies and stay updated on her projects, or drop her a line at bess@steampunkparliament.com to request custom art, design, illustrated book covers, writing and modeling services.

K. Gray is a Southern Californian residing in Southeastern Michigan, hiding from the desert sun for as long as she can. Her endeavors have included teaching, singing, and spending way too much time on the internet. She enjoys all manner of things under the nerd umbrella, long walks on the beach, and forcefully cuddling her dog. Follow her on Twitter @kgraywrites.

Thomas Gregory is an author, performer, and playwright from Southeast Michigan. His Lovecraftian star sign is that of Shub-Niggurath, The Black Goat of the Woods with a Thousand Young.

Aaron Isett was born and raised in Columbus, Ohio. He grew up in the world of fiction, and does his best to reside there as often as possible. He enjoys boxing, cycling, and getting lost in adventure. Follow him on Twitter @g_isett.

Victoria L. Szulc is a multi-media steampunk artist and writer from St. Louis, Missouri. Her works include 2D and 3D visual art in a variety of media, fashion, public art pieces, her steampunk novels of *The Society Series* on Amazon/Kindle, her blog, mysteampunkproject.wordpress.com, and she is a contributing writer to Steampunk Journal. She believes that there is no life without risk, and you haven't lived until you have a few scars.

www.ingramcontent.com/pod-product-compliance
Lightning Source LLC
Chambersburg PA
CBHW021433110726
47901CB00008B/2409